Rainy Season

Rainy Season

Adele Griffin

Houghton Mifflin Company • Boston 1996

For information about this and other Houghton Mifflin trade and reference
books and multimedia products, visit
The Bookstore at Houghton Mifflin on the World Wide Web
at http://www.hmco.com/trade/.

The text of this book is set in 12 point Janson.

Library of Congress Cataloging-in-Publication Data

Griffin, Adele.
Rainy season / Adele Griffin.
p.   cm.
Summary: While living on an army base on the
Panama Canal Zone in 1977, twelve-year-old Lane tries
to cope with the aftermath of a fatal car crash.
ISBN 0-395-81181-3
[1. Death — Fiction. 2. Military bases — Fiction.
3. Canal Zone — Fiction. 4. Panama — Fiction.]
I. Title. PZ7.G881325Rai   1996
[Fic] — dc20   96-121   CIP   AC

Printed in the United States of America
BP   10   9   8   7   6   5   4   3   2   1

For my grandparents, James and Adele Sands

*Special thanks to my agent, Christina Arneson
and my editor, Margaret Raymo*

1

"Charlie!" I shout in a scratchy morning voice. "You up?" There's no answer through the wall that divides our bedrooms. Then I remember; it's Friday. Charlie's been awake for hours.

I've been sleeping too long and my legs feel rubbery when I jump out of bed to shut off the air conditioner. That's a house rule — air conditioners are allowed on during sleeping time only. Mom says they still don't know the long-term effects of Freon in people's lungs. I shove open my window and lean out into the morning, whistling — one long low note and two short ones — and I listen for my bird. He answers back, which I always think is the sign of a good day. I pick my bookmarked Nancy Drew mystery off my nightstand before heading downstairs to breakfast.

Marita and Charlie are slumped around the kitchen table. Charlie's dressed in droopy army fatigue pants and my Spirit of '76 T-shirt. Dad's metal dog tags hang around his neck and two smudges of olive are painted under his eyes.

"You look like a dork." I scowl at him, sliding into my seat. "Plus that's my T-shirt. And Dad's told you a million times, don't use his camouflage stick or wear his ID tags."

"Shut up, Lane. Just because you're too lazy to do the Friday five-mile run with Bravo Company doesn't mean —"

"Oh right, the day I want to wake up at four in the morning and tag along behind a bunch of soldiers."

"Doesn't mean you have to be queen of the rules the minute you —"

"*¿Quieres fruta?*" Marita lifts her eyes from her paperback and points with her chin at the glass fruit bowl.

"She keeps trying to get me to eat that — junk," Charlie grumbles, pushing the glass bowl of papaya, kiwi, mango, and pineapple chunks to the opposite edge of the table from where he's sitting.

"What's wrong with it?" I check out the fruit. "Looks okay to me."

"*Es perfecta.*" Marita lifts the bowl and plunks it firmly in front of Charlie.

"I–don't–want–it." Charlie spaces out his words,

acting as if Marita doesn't understand. "I–hate–jun–gull–fruit."

"*No la quiere,*" I explain, although Marita knows exactly what Charlie's saying, "*No le gusta.*"

"Besides, I had like three bowls of Cheerios already. I'm full." Charlie burps, a gross fat gulp like a bullfrog.

"That's disgusting," I say.

"That's life," he answers smugly, knowing exactly how annoying he's being.

"Where's Mom and Dad?" I ask. "Charlie, I wish you'd've put the milk back in the fridge. Now it's been out too long for my Cheerios to taste good." I pick up the milk carton and shake it. "And there's hardly any left. Thanks a lot."

"I wouldn't've if I'd known you were ever going to wake up, Sleeping Ugly. Anyhow, I need my carbos after a workout with the troops."

"You know, I bet they laugh at you all dressed up in Dad's —"

"Well, at least I'm not a wimpy —"

"Charlie, *por favor* — this fruit is good for you. Will make you strong." Marita doubles her arm and makes a muscle, then jabs her finger at the fruit bowl.

"No way, *gracias.*"

"I'll have some, considering there's practically no milk for cereal." I glare at Charlie and slide into my place. Marita smiles and begins to ladle out a small dish of fruit for me. When she's not looking, Charlie pokes out his tongue at her and rolls his eyes, and I try not to laugh.

The morning heat sticks my nightgown to my legs and my feet to the linoleum floor.

"Don't forget Ted's coming by sometime today to help us build the war fort," Charlie says. "Not that you'll do much good, ye old scrawny arms."

"I know he's coming." I add the last of the warm milk to my Cheerios and shake in some more sugar. Warm, bottom-of-the-carton milk really makes me mad. "Ted called *me*, remember? *I* was the one who told *you*."

Charlie always tries to act like he's better friends with Ted, although I'm actually closer to Ted's age. Charlie's just turned eleven, which makes him two years younger than Ted and over a year younger than me. Charlie's taller, though; a fact that has annoyed me ever since it happened last year.

"Sor-*ry*, know-it-all. When's he coming?"

"Sometime."

" 'Cause what if I want to go to Coronado today?"

"What if? Plenty of kids'll be around to help build even if you're not." My answer doesn't make Charlie happy since he always needs to feel like a big shot.

"Ted told me yesterday that we can get some good quality scrap lumber down by Río Abajo."

"Ted told everyone that when we were at the beach."

"Yeah but he told *me* that he'd take *me* with him to haul it on his truck. 'Cause I'm bigger and stronger." Charlie stretches his arms up over his head like Rocky.

"And dumber."

"I know you are but what am I?"

"Gee, that's a new one." I wash down the heel of a papaya with a sip of orange juice and spread open my Nancy Drew to read. Nancy and her friends have just gone undercover as belly dancers to uncover some missing ancient jewels; I started the book last night and I'm already halfway done.

Charlie and I haven't been in school all week, because on Monday the Fort Bryan school gym and part of the music department flooded from the rains. They closed the school for repairs until next Monday, so most kids, including Charlie and me, have been spending every day at either Fort Hastings pool, Coronado, or Kobbe Beach. Today's Friday, the last day of our surprise vacation, and I'll almost be glad to get back to school. So much time hanging out in the sun with Charlie, and even with Nancy Drew, is getting kind of boring.

The two kitchen fans; one on the table, one wedged onto the windowsill, stir up the warm air in their paths but barely relieve the heat. I scoot my chair closer to the table fan and lean my face into the trickle of moving air.

"Hello hello, I'm home. Who's here?" Dad used to sing in a rock and roll band when he was in college, and I can always hear the smooth undersong in his voice. His combat boots clomp down the long hall to the kitchen, following Charlie's voice yelping, "In here, we're all in here, Dad!"

"*¿Dónde está la Señora?*" he asks Marita while Charlie lunges over to him, jumping up and snatching off Dad's Special Forces beret, which he snaps over his own head.

"*Con Alexa,*" Marita answers, and then in English adds, "shopping." The way she says it, the word sounds like "chopping." She starts setting a breakfast place for Dad.

"They go into Panama City?" Dad asks. He pours himself some coffee but won't take a seat. Dad's not a sit-down-and-smell-the-coffee kind of person. His eyes squint out the window over the sink. He's been inside for only a minute and I can tell he wants to zip out again.

"*Sí,*" Marita nods. Dad turns to me, frowning, his eyebrows quirked into question marks.

"Lane, when did Mom go downtown? Did she say when she'd be back?"

"I've only been up for like five minutes."

"Hey, Dad, I did the five-mile run with Bravo, and guess what Sergeant Brady told me?" Charlie speaks just under shouting level, then launches into a long story about how Sergeant Brady thought Charlie should go out for track or be in the Olympics or some dumb thing. I raise my head from my book to look at Dad.

"Be quiet a second, Charlie. Dad, is something happening downtown?"

"There was a radio advisory bulletin about some disturbances, but if Mom's with Alexa I'm not worried. They'll be back any minute. So no histrionics, please." Dad winks at me, but I'm already on my feet.

"So, anyhow, Sergeant Brady wanted me to ask you if —"

"Dad, can I call the MP's? Just to ask how safe it is? Just to make sure everything's okay?"

"Oh good grief, Lane, no. And sit down. *¡Qué dramáticos!*" Dad smiles at Marita, but then asks her something in Spanish. I only recognize a few words: danger, cars, looking; but it's enough to make me feel sick to my stomach. Marita just shrugs, mumbles something I don't understand, and keeps reading.

"I hope Mom wasn't wearing jewelry. Ted says that if you're wearing jewelry and you go into some parts of Panama City, the locals'll chop off your fingers to steal your rings." Charlie snips the air with his fingers. "Or maybe they're shooting at MP patrols again." He starts making spitty machine gun noises.

"Shut up, Charlie." I press my palms against my scalp, trying to make myself think clearly. "This is bad. This is really bad." Dad rolls his eyes. I start pacing up and down the length of the kitchen. "You have to get in there, Dad, and find her before it's too late."

"Lane, the only thing I might have to do is give you an Academy Award for this charming performance." Dad sighs. "Don't you think that if I were really worried, I would call the MP's myself? Hmm? Look at me, Lane. It wasn't even a real warning; just a bulletin. I bet Charlie's right — some local kid was probably taking a crack shot at a military patrol car. No big deal. I should never have said anything."

He has to call out that last part because I'm already running down the long hall that separates the kitchen from the rest of the house, upstairs, and into my bedroom, where I slam the door behind me. I click my clock radio to the military station to listen for police updates and then, since I don't have much of a direct plan, I pull out my journal from its hiding place under my mattress.

Emily gave me the journal a long time ago, when we lived in the States. The picture on the cover shows a girl sitting in the middle of a tulip with a quill pen poised in her hand. Emily said the girl looked like me. I flip to the next blank page and write:

Dear Emily,

Today Mom disappeared, and Dad doesn't even care.

She went downtown with Alexa this morning, and has not been heard from since.

If something ever happens to Mom, then I am going to go back to the States and live with Mina and Pops.

It starts taking too long thinking up the next sentence, so I shove the journal under some books on my desk and crawl into bed, worming into the covers, where I concentrate on wishing that Mom would come home. *Be-safe, be-safe,* I whisper to myself, like in meditation class. I try to imagine Dr. Forrest in her crooked lipstick and holding her brown clipboard. Sometimes picturing Dr. Forrest calms me down a little. I close my eyes, trying to lull myself to sleep so I don't have to think.

A few minutes later, I hear Dad's feet on the stairs and then he knocks on my door. When I don't answer he clears his throat and says, "I'm taking off work this morning to go watch the paratroopers and I'm bringing Charlie. You want to come with?"

"I'm waiting for Mom in case she calls and needs my help."

"Have it your way then, Miss Housecat."

"Dad, what if she's really in trouble and we need to rescue her out of downtown?"

"When has that ever happened, Lane?"

I don't answer him. He should know that anyplace off-base is unpredictable. Locals hate American military. "Gringos go home!" graffiti is sprayed over enough off-base bus stop benches and bridge underpasses for me to get the message.

Charlie and Dad leave in the jeep. Marita goes with them, getting a lift to the PX to do some shopping. She skews her eyes up to my window, although the blinds hide me. I bet she thinks I'm *loca*, a crazy. For a second I want to run out to join them.

"Please be safe, Mom. Please be safe," I whisper. But underneath this fresh worry, memories of the accident are beginning to buckle and shake me. I fight them, hard. "Be-safe be-safe," I say, louder, to stop my thoughts.

I turn up my radio so that it blares its update of which movies are playing in the theaters across the bases. It doesn't help, but even through my fears I'm mad at myself, for not going to see the paratroopers, for letting my imagination run away with me for the millionth time. It's not like I can pretend I don't know why I get like this. It's just I don't know exactly how to stop.

2

Half an hour later, the doorbell chimes. I'd been lying in bed, but I'm at my window in a flash. There's no car. If Mom got crushed in a riot downtown, I'd have seen the MP's black military jeep. Still, I sprint downstairs to the front door, expecting the worst.

"Hey, Lane-brain." Ted Tie grins from the porch step. "You guys ready?"

"Ted. Hey."

"Charlie coming, too?" Ted's holding his large tool kit with **Ted Tie — Touch and Die!** magic-markered in black across the top.

"Charlie's not here and I can't leave the house."

"Where is he?" Ted strolls past me into the living room. "Got any Pepsi? It's getting crispy hot outside." He plops into the loveseat, sets his toolbox beside him, and yanks up his T-shirt to wipe the sweat off his face.

"Ted, you have to move that — no, not on the carpet." I lift the toolbox off the rug and set it on the floor tile. Maybe it's because Ted is almost fourteen and thinks he's as good as any adult, or maybe it's because he's always lived on the Panama Canal Zone — a Zonian, like Alexa — but he never puts any effort into being polite.

Zonians are what everyone calls Americans who live in the Panama Canal Zone, a U.S. owned strip of land that runs right through the middle of Panama, from the Atlantic to the Pacific. Zonians are non-military Americans who have moved down here over the past hundred years, to work for the Pan-Canal Company. The Zone's a kind of wild, carefree place and since Zonians have Panamanian as well as U.S. citizenship they don't much care for U.S. rules and regulations.

"So why aren't you coming to build the fort? We really need you on the front lines. I hear those kids from the other side have their fort almost totally finished."

"Listen, have you heard about anything bad happening downtown this morning? Mom and Alexa went shopping earlier and they're not back."

"Aw, you know it's just local kids stealing whatever — *las ruedas*, abandoned car parts — those military radio bulletins always exaggerate. Can you or Marita fix me a Pepsi? I'm parched."

"Marita's at the PX and Dad and Charlie went to the jump — and Ted, I'm getting really worried about Mom. It's almost eleven. She left — I don't know — maybe around eight or nine, I was still sleeping, but Dad's gone and so it's all up to me to wait and see —"

"Earth to Lane. This little story's getting mighty boring, besides emphasizing that you're a total grapenut. I'm gonna go grab that Pepsi myself. Wanta glass?"

"No, and we only have ginger ale."

"Fine by me." Ted is already down the hall. While he's gone I move his grimy toolbox into the front hall, where the floor is just plain linoleum.

Ted notices as soon as he comes back. "You and your fussy family. Jeez," he sighs, flopping back onto the loveseat, the quart-sized ginger ale bottle cradled in his palm, "I don't know why the Duchess gets so bent out of shape about a little mess."

"She just likes everything in its place," I say.

"And she's always been a neat freak? That'd drive me crazy."

I have to think for a minute. "Well, when we lived in Virginia, at Fort Pershing, we didn't have a dishwasher, so sometimes plates stacked up in the sink. But just sometimes."

Ted narrows his eyes and runs his tongue over his

bottom lip like he's tasting my answer. "Hey, lemme see a picture of Virginia. Where's Virginia, anyway? Near Miami?"

"Um, not really." I lean over and pull the photo album off the coffee table, then set myself next to Ted on the loveseat. The album cover is cranberry-dark leather with the photographs hand-glued to soft charcoal-colored pages on the inside.

"This is so out of touch," Ted comments, flipping past the fuzzy black and white pictures of old relatives to the modern colored photos. "It's cracked. Who wants to see like the whole history of your family from the Dark Ages? And has the Duchess ever heard of those plastic picture separators? You know, with the sticky —"

"There, that's my grandparents' house in Virginia," I point.

Ted studies the picture for a while. "Lots o' trees. My grandparents used to live in a big old house in Germany before they lived here."

"Why'd they leave Germany?"

Ted shrugs. "Guess they kind of had to, since it was World War II and probably the whole entire country was getting bombed. Next time I go up to Miami, I'll ask them. Ha — is that the Duchess in the poufy wig?"

"I think that's just how they wore their hair in those

times." Seeing the picture of Mom reminds me. "Ted, don't you think we should call the MP's?"

"What?" Ted looks up at me and frowns. "No way, she's fine. Stop hyperventilating about it. Why are some of these pictures all cut up and weird looking?"

I peer into the book. "Where?"

He points. "There. And that one."

"Oh, Mom just does that so if someone looks bad in the picture, like red eyes or blurry or something, she'll cut that part out and keep the good part of the picture in. So that the whole picture isn't ruined."

Ted looks at me skeptically. "See, that's just what I'm talking about. Fussiness." He slaps the album shut. "I think I just heard a car door slam."

I leap to the window and once I see that it's Mom and Alexa, I can feel my worries squeeze out of me like hot water from a washcloth.

"Why are you being so friendly?" Mom asks with a smile. As soon as she walks inside, I have her in a clutch; it's babyish and I know Ted and Alexa are watching, but I bury my face in her shoulder. Mom sets down her shopping bags and returns my hug, although her eyes quiz me.

"I thought there was trouble downtown. Dad told me." I let go of her; Mom crosses her arms over her chest and shakes her head.

"Well, it's sweet of you to be concerned, Lanie, but we both know very well that this is exactly the kind of thing . . ." Her voice dies away at the sight of Ted, who waves at her from the loveseat.

"Heya, Duchess."

"Well, if it isn't Mr. Tie!" Mom's face relaxes back into a smile and she nods to his drink. "No beverages on the furniture."

"Argghhh." Ted stands, resting his weight on one leg, then tips back his head and drains the bottle like he's on a television commercial.

"Theodore, doesn't Dee have enough bread and water that you don't have to schlep around here on the dole?" asks Alexa, settling herself carefully into a spindly-legged chair.

"Dee's an unfit mother," Ted smirks. "You should know — you trained her."

Alexa laughs in a giant rumble. Ted's mom Dee and Alexa used to be something wild growing up on the Zone — I've heard lots of crazy stories. She and Dee and their Zonie friends were always up to strange things like water-skiing through the Pedro Miguel locks or racing their jeeps over the Fort Davidson golf course.

"You are so brutal to me, Teddy Tie. Isn't it Friday today? Why aren't you in school? Rain didn't blow down the doors over at *Escuela Balboa* too, did it?"

"It's called a sick day, Alexa. More interesting things to do than geometry, right?" Ted jams the hands of his crossed arms under his armpits and lifts his shoulders and his eyebrows. "Just don't tell Dee. I'm thinking you can keep a secret."

"Well, stop thinking. And why do I have a feeling you've put in for a whole sick week?" Alexa shakes a finger at him, but it wouldn't even cross her mind to tell Dee. Dee doesn't care whether Ted goes to class or the beach; one thing I've learned here is that school isn't so much taught on the Zone as it's just tolerated, like the rains.

"So Ted, what's the lowdown on Jennifer Elwig — or do you have a new flavor of the week?" Alexa is always way too curious about everybody's love life.

"Believe me, I'm still smitten. She's old, though — two years too old for me. I might call her if I'm feeling deliriously brave," Ted jokes. "Since you and the Duchess both are taken."

"Oh you hush, you bad thing." Alexa turns her head and flutters her eyes. It's plain that she likes his flattery, though, which makes me feel kind of sorry for her and kind of amazed.

It's weird how parents and other grownups love Ted. It's partly because he's nice to look at — tall and tan with gold flecks in his hair and eyes. Mostly though, he's just so comfortable inside himself that he brings out a comfortable feeling in other people. Ted's a kid you always meet with exclamation points — "Hey! It's the man! Tie! Whatsup, Ted! — even if you don't normally speak that way.

Mom never even minds that he calls her the Duchess. He named her from his poster of David Bowie, who Ted told me sometimes is called the Thin White Duke. I've seen that poster in his room, and Ted's right, Mom looks just like it: she's long and flat and pale, with prickly yellow hair and a bony face like a greyhound dog, like David Bowie. Mom also wears men's clothes; always flared jeans and pantsuits and button-down shirts. No makeup, either. The only time I ever saw her wear a really nice dress was in photos from when she and Dad got married. She says pants are her rebellion against her Virginia upbringing, when she had to wear skirts and pantyhose, even on the weekends.

Alexa is Mom's opposite; she wears sparkly eyeshadow and her long black hair looks like it was carved into its polished knot. Alexa also likes to dress in floor-length swishy things. Today the swishy thing is green and it sticks to her body like Plasti-Rap. The whole effect reminds me of a peeled avocado.

"Where're the men?" Mom asks.

"At the jump. Marita's out, shopping." Now I'm

sort of depressed that I didn't go to the jump when I had the chance.

Alexa looks crabby. "Marita's not here? Then we'll have to go out, Abby, like to the Officer's Club." She pats her stomach. "I'm famished."

"Don't be crazy," Mom starts heading to the kitchen. "You forget *I'm* from the U.S. of A. I still know how to slap a piece of cheese between two slices of bread."

Alexa wrinkles her nose and starts to say something, but then stops and turns to Ted. "So is Dee on for the party tonight?"

"There's a party here tonight?" Ted looks at me.

"I didn't know," I say. We both turn to Alexa, who laughs.

"That's because Abby and I decided on it this morning."

"Is that enough time to get all the food ready?"

"Oh no, no, no, silly girl — we're having it catered. It's someone else's problem — we just show up, eat, and go home!" Alexa starts really cracking up now, although no one else is joining in. "But I do need to get on the horn and ring up the gang." She sighs when she recovers.

"Hey, Lane, we should go see the jump," Ted says. "Dee and Grant took the Toyota to the Atlantic side to go scuba diving, so we've got Grant's truck for the whole day. And we can recruit more builders while we're over at McKenna."

"I need to change first. I'm still in my nightgown."

"Hurry up then. Day's wasting."

"Ten minutes." I sprint to my room to get ready before Ted becomes impatient and takes off without me, which he's been known to do in true Zonie style.

3

I take a cold shower to get ready for the heat, then I pull on my bathing suit and a cotton sundress. My sandals, once white, are still pretty damp from when I stomped them through yesterday's rain puddles. I squish them on anyway.

I sit on my bed and try scraping a comb through my wet hair. Once Emily told me I had thick movie star hair, although all I see is mouse brown to match my mouse gray eyes. Sometimes, right after I'd washed it, she'd wind it into a French braid. When it dried, she'd unravel the braid into bumps and waves.

There's a picture somewhere; me in a movie star pose with my unbraided hair spread all over my shoulders, and then Emily in the back holding a bottle of hairspray and wearing a cowboy hat, pretending to be the Hairdresser to the Stars. "Dahling, you must stop by my saloon!" she scribbled on the corner of the picture. Sometimes I wonder if she spelled it saloon because of the cowboy hat, or had meant to write salon like a hair salon. Either way, it's funny.

I'll have to finish the letter I started writing to her in my journal. It's been almost a month since I wrote a letter to Emily.

I give up on the comb, wiggling my fingers down through the knots and snags as I rejoin the others in the living room.

"I'm ready."

Ted jumps up and swipes another half of cheese sandwich from the platter Mom must have prepared. "Let's motor. Got your pass?"

I pat the side slit pocket of my dress.

"Lane, when you see Dad, will you tell him about tonight but ask him *please* don't invite anyone yet, since Alexa and I are still making the list?" Mom points a warning finger at me.

"Okay."

"And drive carefully, Ted," she adds. She's still not used to the idea that Zonians don't think they need to be a certain age to drive. Military kids, like me, all have to follow the laws of the American government. No questions asked. But Ted's lucky; even though he's an American citizen, living on the Panama Canal Zone is pretty different from living on an army base.

The whole Zone's nearly 650 square miles. And

while the 14 bases built along the Zone are all very regulated and orderly, the Zone has real neighborhoods, with lawns and garages and barbecue grills. As far as neighborhoods go, they're pretty average-American looking, except for being built in the middle of the jungle, and most Zonians are more likely to keep boats, trucks and jeeps in their garages, instead of cars.

Almost everyone who lives on the Zone works for the government, mostly for the Pan-Canal Company. Ted's dad, Grant, is a lock-switch operator. Ted only ever leaves Panama to see his grandparents in Miami. Almost all Zonians, once they retire from the Pan-Canal Company, go live in Miami. Ted thinks the whole United States is like Miami — full of mini-golf ranges and old people.

We walk outside, down the front steps and into the shadowless heat. Ted swings his toolbox and whistles. The black plaque, stamped out like a license plate and fixed to our front door screen — #4J Lt. Col. Beck — is the one thing that distinguishes our house from all the others on First Street.

Ted looks up. "Gonna rain today."

I look up, too. "Negative."

"Around four. You watch."

I give the sky a double-check and decide Ted is *loco*.

All the houses on our street are built to look exactly

alike; white-walled, double-decked plaster-and-concrete boxes with black metal roofs. Only the General's house is bigger. It's at the very end of the road, shaped like three sides of a rectangle and half-hidden behind a prickly hedge and an unfriendly square iron gate. Dad says that military architecture is uninspired, but I like the exactness of all the straight, clean lines.

We skitter down the steep hill to the bottom of the base and I nod and wave to the MP on duty in the control box. Ted salutes, which seems a little bit obnoxious, but very Ted-ish. His truck is parked at the bottom of the hill. It doesn't have a military pass sticker, since the truck belongs to his dad, so Ted has to park it off-base. You need a pass sticker to drive onto any military base here, and you need an ID card if you want to buy anything from a U.S. government store. It's strict down here, because the country is in what Dad calls "uneasy time," especially now with President Jimmy Carter about to give the rights to the Canal over to the Panamanian government. Panama is the first place I've lived where I feel that I fit in on the base, but I don't belong anywhere else; not downtown and especially not on the Zone.

"Hot seats," Ted warns. "Towel in the pit."

I dig out the towel and fold it over the vinyl before sitting.

"This thing's such an old hunk of junk." I sigh as

the truck rattles onto the strip. "Plus it smells like hamburgers."

"This beauty? This is a priceless '66 Ford pick-up you're talking about — only one year younger than you."

"Too old."

"Yeah, well, so's this stupid road," Ted grumbles as the truck clanks over a pothole. "Anything that's non-military gets low priority around here, I'm telling you. Makes me think about joining the army sometimes. Live on a cushy base like Fort Bryan."

"You'd make the worst soldier, Ted. For one, you'd always be trying to get out of doing work and stuff."

"So how does that make me different from anyone else in any other job?" He laughs. "I wonder if I'd be a good construction worker, though. I'd like to learn for myself how to fill some of these potholes."

We bounce and jolt along the roads that separate Fort Bryan from Fort McKenna. The intersections are swarming with slow-walking venders carrying plastic bags of plantains, limes, and scraggly lettuces. Little boys holding sponges and buckets run to the stopped cars, trying to wash a windshield for a quarter.

"*Váyate.*" Ted bats his hand out the window. I dig in my side pocket and pull out some change; the boys grab for my money.

"Lane, come on." Ted snaps. "You give one quarter

to one local, you get twenty more holding out their hands. It's like seagulls." I know it's nothing like sea-gulls, but I keep quiet. Sometimes Ted talks thought-less like that.

Ted turns onto a back road to get to McKenna; it's just a strip of dirt that cuts through the jungle. The riding's actually smoother once we hit the red-packed soil. We drive by a girl and boy, each lugging two plastic milk containers filled with water. The girl stares unsmilingly at our truck but the boy raises one hand and waves and some of his water sloshes out onto the road. I wave back at him. Ted looks irked.

"Wasn't that local kid asking for a lift?"

"I think he was just waving."

"They all want lifts, and then they'll steal your wal-let while they're saying thanks for the ride. You shouldn't've waved."

"Oh, how many Panamanian kids do you know who have done that to you, stolen stuff from you?" I ask him. Ted scrunches his nose.

"None, but I just know. Locals, man. They hate the Zone and they hate military worse. Think they own the country, just cause they were here first."

"But they do own —"

"Oh, they do not, not really. They own barely anything."

"They'll own the Canal now."

"That's a good one. You think the U.S. is really going to hand over the Canal to Panama? It's just a lot of talk, Lane." Ted speeds up the truck so that we go flying over a bump and I try to laugh even though going fast always makes me feel sick.

Today marks the second week of November, almost the bottom of 1977. In Rhode Island, where we lived before here, November means cold — a month of bleak sunlight icing the dead grass on our lawn. Down here, November is the rainy season, which means feeling slow and dumb from heat until we're soaked by the violent relief of a dark afternoon downpour. Right now, though, the sun is screaming hot.

"We live on one of the most boring bases on the Pacific side," I sigh. "Mom always says the Pacific side's better than the Atlantic side, since the Pacific side's close to Panama City with all the good shopping and restaurants. But Fort Bryan's dull."

Ted nods. "Yeah, well, it's a small base. No room for jump grounds or a high school, or a PX or dinner theater like there is on McKenna. But if I had to live on a base, I'd rather do the Atlantic side thing. Gotta love the Caribbean; way better beaches, way cooler scuba."

"Ugh, I'll never scuba dive — all those scary fish faces up close."

"Lane-insane." Ted shakes his head. "If they took the word scary out of your vocab, you'd be a mute."

We turn off-road just before Fort McKenna, bumping down the side of a hill so fast that I grip the dashboard. We park just outside the base again, and the walk to the McKenna jump field is enough of a stretch that by the time Dad waves us over, Ted and I are both glazed with sweat.

It looks like almost a hundred people have collected on the field to watch the jump. Everywhere, families lounge on blankets spread over the stubbly grass. A batch of little kids churn up and down the far edge of the field, trying to work a Chinese Dragon kite into the air.

Ted cups his hands over his mouth. "Too much string, kite people!" he yells. "Goofy little squirts," he says to me.

"Ted!" Dad smiles. He's sprawled out on a poncho liner. He raises his hand so that Ted can smack him with a high-five.

"Where's Charlie?" I ask. My eyes scan the sun-burnt turf.

"Went to find a bathroom," Dad says. His eyes are resting on the sky and his hands are propped behind his head. "Sit down, you. I guess Mom made it back in one piece?" He's teasing me, but I don't smile. I'm thinking of other things. Last time Charlie and I went

to a jump, Charlie swore he'd figure out a way to get
Major Brandt to take him up in a plane. My nerves are
already jangling.

"When did Charlie leave?" I ask.

"Lane, come on. You heard your dad." Ted throws
himself stomach-down on the poncho and reaches up
to tug the hem of my dress. "Sit down with us. It's so
pathetic when you do this."

"It's just that last time we went to a jump, he
said —"

"We're not listening to you, Sarah Bernhardt," says
Dad. "Take a seat."

I drop with a huff, cross-legged, onto the poncho
liner. Dad and Mom sometimes call me Sarah Bernhardt, who was some outdated, overdramatic French
actress. Since I never saw any Sarah Bernhardt movies,
I don't exactly see the humor and Dad's comment just
makes me mad.

When I was younger, I liked it when people would
remark that I was like seeing Dad all over again. I like
the way we can find the upper harmony to any song
on the radio and know how to throw a Frisbee perfectly flat and how we both write out daily schedules
on index cards in one color and then cross each thing
off in another color.

Now I stare at my dad's profile and think about how
old he looks. Little tinselly strands of gray sparkle

through his dark crew cut, and an age line hooks a path from his nose down to his mouth. I try to imagine him skinny and playing guitar in his college band. I try to picture him calling Mom up for a date, and Mom being all excited and writing her name plus his name with a heart around it, like Rachel Orndorf who's in my grade and always does that with anyone she thinks is cute.

"I can feel you scowling at me." Dad speaks without looking my direction. "Watch the sky instead; you're about to miss it."

"I am not scowling at you."

"Watch the sky."

I lift my chin higher to absorb the sky. Suddenly I see the jump plane; it's outline jags a black scar across the thin blue skin of the horizon. I hold my breath as the paratroopers drop, shapeless blots at first like a spray of pea gravel, until their chutes pop and release, billowing into silk bubbles above the specks of the soldier's bodies. Now they're easily visible, sinking without noise through the distant air.

"Charlie's missing it, wherever he may be." I address Dad, who doesn't react. "Wherever he may be," I repeat. "Which is not here." Dad's just staring across the field. I follow his eyes to spot Charlie, who's sprinting toward us. His bad leg kicks out crooked to the side as he runs, like a stork. For a minute Dad's face looks shocked and sad, and I wonder if Charlie's leg is making him think back to the accident.

"Charlie," he shouts. "Over here!" I squint, something's not right in Charlie's face. He's moving fast across the ground, eyes trained on Dad, and his face is twisted up.

"My knees," he hollers once he's in earshot. "I skidded in the parking lot."

"Oh good grief." Dad climbs to his feet, brushing the grass from his hands. "Lane, stay put, okay? As much as I love watching your hysterics at the sight of blood . . ." He heads off in a half trot across the field.

"Charlie-horse is one reckless fellow." Ted laughs. "Should *I* go help?"

"No, Dad's got it." He's crouched down now, examining Charlie's knees.

"What happened to Charlie?" Ted and I turn at the voice behind us.

"Steph, take a seat." Ted points to the space on the poncho where Dad had been lying.

"Hi, Steph." I flutter my fingers in a wave. "He scraped his knees or something. Are you here with your folks?"

"My mom's over there." Steph points vaguely behind her and plops down, squeezing into the narrow space between Ted and me. She looks up at the sky. "My dad's jumping today. He already went."

"Wow, Steph, guess you make a tasty feast." Ted pokes his finger against one of Steph's white legs, which are scattered with blooming pink mosquito bites.

"No kidding. My blood must be gourmet." Steph presses one of her fingers onto Ted's leg. "All you ever get's a tan, Zonie."

"Steph, remember you're building the fort with us later on today," Ted tells her.

"No problemo. Coronado and Kobbe are getting so old. Besides, you should see the fort those winky kids from the other side have built. It's got a chained door and everything. Rat and I sneaked over to see it the other night."

Rat Wagner is Steph's twin brother. His real name is Ray. They're both in my grade but they fight so much in school that for two years in a row they had to be assigned seats at opposite sides of the classroom. Out of school, Steph and Rat usually stick together like two sides of a coin, although I wouldn't say they get along, exactly. But at least when they're not in school one won't put the other in a headlock over who can do fractions faster or exactly why General Lee lost the battle of Gettysburg.

"Where is the Rat, anyway?" Ted asks.

Steph runs her hand through her rusted-iron colored hair. "He killed a fruit bat," she exhales all at once, like a confession. "I mean, it must have been sick or something anyway, since it was in plain sight, just lying in our carport this morning. Rat thought it was a rock because he didn't have his glasses on when he went out to get the paper and he stepped on it and killed it — squished it to death." Steph makes a noise that I guess is supposed to be the sound of a bat getting squished.

"That's so sad." I chew at the skin around my fingernails. "Poor little bat."

"What's worse is Rat was barefoot. He's really upset about the whole thing."

Ted sort of chokes through his nose and it sounds a lot like a laugh. Steph lifts her eyebrows at him, then continues.

"So he's home making a coffin and digging a grave for Robin — that's what he named the bat. I have to go back home soon for the funeral. You know how Rat gets so upset about that kind of stuff, like last summer when those little kids at Fort Hastings were squishing up butterflies to see if they had yellow blood, remember how Rat yelled at them and called all their parents on the phone?"

I nod. "I'll come back with you, if you want. To go to the funeral." I feel sorry for the little dead fruit bat, but also sorry for poor old Rat. He acts tough around the edges, but he's pretty soft in the middle, especially about animals. Softer than Steph, who probably would have put the blame on the bat if she'd been the one to step on it.

"Great. Let me ask my mom if you can come for lunch. Ted, you wanna come too?"

"Actually, I have to get stuff for the fort." When Steph had mentioned how good the other side's fort was, Ted got all clenched up. Suddenly he jumps to a stand and walks away from us over to Dad and Charlie.

Steph pushes her lips out like a fish, watching him go. "I think the sky show's almost over," she says. "I'm gonna ask my mom about lunch. Be right back." She darts away, less interested in hanging around since Ted isn't with us. I stretch out flat on my back on the poncho and close my eyes, letting the sun lash down on me, the strength of its heat planting me into the ground, into sleep. Dr. Forrest used to say that calm moments were better times than crises for meditation, so in my head I start repeating my secret meditation word *vi-ta*, *vi-ta*, very slow, the way they taught me at the center.

"Check out my knees!" I open my eyes to see Charlie's standing right over me. "Especially the left one." The puffy scab on his left knee from when he fell off his bike last week is split open in a thin crooked line, leaking a smear of fresh blood.

I sit up and scoot away from him crabways. "Cut it out, it makes me sick." Charlie touches some of the blood to his fingers, then flashes them in my face.

"Doesn't hurt at all."

I smack his hand away. "Looks disgusting."

"You can come!" Steph bounces up to me. She looks over at Dad, who's standing a few feet away, talking to Ted, and cleaning his glasses with the corner of his T-shirt. "Ask," she hisses. She grabs at my hand and pulls, yanking me up to my feet.

"Dad, can I go to Steph's for lunch?"

"Her mother knows?"

"Mom knows. Charlie and Ted can come too." Steph grins doubtfully at Ted, preparing for failure again, but it's her nature to press a point.

"Charlie and I are going to pick up lumber. We'll stop at the McDonald's on the Zone." He speaks to Dad as if double-checking. Ted must have already run the plan by him. "We'll come by after lunch to pick you both up — I can go on base since Lord Beck just gave me this military vehicle day pass." Ted opens his fist to display Dad's blue guest pass card, then shoves it deep in his shorts' pocket. Steph looks down and scuffs the grass with the toe of her sneaker; she's disappointed and it makes me mad. I feel like the consolation prize lunch guest.

"Dad, I forgot to tell you. Mom and Alexa are having a party at our house tonight."

"Well, I hope she didn't forget about the change of command party we have to — Aha, Captain!" Dad smiles as Steph's dad joins our circle, dragging his half-packed parachute in his rucksack. He's outfitted in his camouflage fatigues and boots. Sloppy half-moons of sweat darken the armpits and chest of his olive green T-shirt. Captain Wagner crisply salutes Dad, who just taps the closed fingers of his hand against his temple. "You looked good out there, Wagner. Easy jump?"

"Yes sir, good day for it."

"We're having a get together tonight at my place if you and Sue want to stop by."

"Will do, sir. Affirmative."

Dad had spilled the invitation before I could tell him about not inviting army people. My eyes try to fire a warning signal to him, but he doesn't get it. He just smiles at me.

"So you're borrowing and feeding my daughter?" Dad asks. "I guess I'll see you later then, Lane. Have fun building your clubhouse. No worrying, that's an order. See you too, Captain." He snaps his fingers and looks at me. "Around what time did Mom say for tonight?"

"I dunno," I mumble.

"I'm guessing nine-ish then, after the change of command ceremony." Dad nods to everyone. "Take care." As I watch him leave I wonder if I should stop him from doing more damage, but since he already told the Wagners, Dad basically opened the party to Army People, which I know is exactly what Mom didn't want. Because if you invite one army couple, others come. I guess I'll just have to tell her.

"Come on, Lane. Everyone's already in the parking lot." Steph starts leaping across the field. I turn away from watching Dad and run to catch up.

4

We sit in the way back of the Wagners' wood-sided station wagon, in the part with no seats, far away from Steph's parents so that we can talk freely about the war fort and the kids from the other side.

"You know Jason McCullough?" Steph lowers her voice and her eyes flit to the front seat, checking to make sure that her parents aren't eavesdropping. She pulls her T-shirt over her knees and then wraps her arms tight around them, folding herself into a box with a head on top and sneakers poking out the bottom.

I shake my head. Steph leans in closer to me.

"He lives over on 6th Street and goes to Fort Bryan West, but he stayed back like three times, and I heard that when the kids from the other side built their war fort it was his idea to bury a machete and a BB-gun in a footlocker underneath the ground. But that could be a lie. But anyhow, you'd maybe remember him from soccer camp."

I think back to the sweaty herds of kids from soccer camp. "Is he, um, really really tall with brown hair in a bowl cut?" I ask.

"No. Well, maybe. He's not that tall and I think he has a buzz cut now. Anyhow, he's a psychopathical — no, wait — pathological liar and once he stole a bike and his dad put him out in the yard on a dog chain to punish him."

"Lie. That's a lie."

Steph looks stricken. With her pinkie, she slices an X across her chest. "Cross my heart, I heard that. This kid is *loco*. Crazier than Charlie."

I ignore that last comment. "What's a pathological liar?"

"Someone who lies because they can't help it; for them a lie is as good as the truth. It's kind of like a disease."

I thought about my family and wondered if this is what had happened to us?

"You girls want macaroni and cheese or peanut-butter-and-jelly?" Mrs. Wagner twists around from the front seat to look at us. She smiles wide, like she can't wait to get started making lunch. Her excitement over things like this is partly why Mom has a problem getting along with her. "She burbles,"

Mom says. Still, Mrs. Wagner's always trying to get Mom over for lunch or a game of racquetball, and Mom always pretends that she has errands or a headache.

"Peanut-butter-and-jelly," Steph and I shout.

"Grape jelly," Steph says.

"Please," I add. Mrs. Wagner smiles even wider, dropping her mouth open.

"Sweet girl," she says to me. "I wish my Stephanie was so polite and sweet."

The Wagners live in Fort Bryan too, but on Fourth Street where all the captains live. I live on a different street because Dad's a lieutenant colonel. The army organizes everything so nobody has any questions. If you know the rank of someone's dad (or mom, but it usually doesn't happen that way), then you pretty much know where the family lives, and the higher ranks get the bigger houses. It's not so different from the regular world; it's just that with the families and ranks divided up as square as a TV dinner, there's less guessing about who has what.

The thing is, I know that Mrs. Wagner wants Steph to be my friend just because of my dad's rank. Even if I liked acid rock music and wore skimpy halter tops, like Major Franken's daughter, Mrs. Wagner would want Steph to be friends with me. Steph and I think it's funny, but then Steph also doesn't seem to go out of her way to make any friends whose dads are lieutenants or privates or even captains like her own dad.

Air conditioners blast night and day in the Wagners' house. Their floors are a spongy blue ocean of carpeting and the house is decorated completely with furniture that they've collected from Captain Wagner's military tours of duty. Most army homes are like that, where you can tell exactly where the officers and their families have been stationed by what they bought while they were there.

At the Wagners', the heavy wood trunk and matching dining room table came from Germany, the wooden screens were brought back from Seoul, Korea, and the oversized Mola pillows and the bamboo chair in the hall are already souvenirs of here. I like recognizing the overseas tours from the furniture. It's like seeing a living history of a family.

Steph and I kick off our shoes at the door and run to Rat's room.

"Your professional mourners are here for the funeral!" Steph yells, pouncing over to where Rat's hunched at his desk. I trail behind and lean in his doorframe, feeling out of place, because I know that he doesn't like people to enter his sacred domain — the Rat-trap, Steph calls it. "My brother's a pack rat," Steph told us when we all first met at the annual Army

Hail and Farewell picnic. "Just call him Rat." And so we do.

Rat's room is so jammed full of stuff that there's almost no place to stand. The blue wall-to-wall peeks out in patches, but mostly it's covered by boxes filled with strange rummage that Rat won't throw out. His bookshelves spill over with papers and paperbacks and science fiction comic books, not to mention his rock collection, shell collection, and rare bottle collection.

Lots of pictures of himself and Steph are hung or taped up like a pattern on the wall. A good one is of the two of them standing together, wearing their Little League softball uniforms. Steph's arm is roped around Rat's neck and it looks almost like she's choking him, but they're both smiling at something and you can even see a little silver dot of filling in the back of Rat's mouth.

"Ever hear of knocking?" Rat growls at us now. "Get out. Steph. Lane. Out." He's holding what looks like a cross made from two sticks, held at the center with a twist of puke-green yarn. "I'm busy."

"We want to help. That's why we're here," Steph wheedles. "You said you needed me to come back."

"I un-need you. I want to do it all myself. You'll just take over the whole thing if I let you in on it."

"I will not! And Lane came specially. It's better for

a funeral if a lot of people show up, so it looks like Robin had a lot of friends."

"Shut up, Steph. You're making fun of me."

"Shut up, Rat. I am not."

"Both of you." I clear my throat. "Come on."

Rat surveys his sister through his army-issue black-rimmed glasses. The awful twist in Steph and Rat's twinship, is that, no matter how you look at it, Rat seems made from whatever was left over after Steph came out. When she told me that she's eighteen minutes and twenty-three seconds older, it only reinforced my secret theory.

Steph got all the appetite; for running and talking and fighting — Rat's quiet, more of a hibernator. Steph's reddish-brown hair and greenish-brown eyes drained into regular old brown on Rat, and his eyes have the double insult of not even working very well. And although he's the one who looks like a perfect candidate for nerd-of-the-month club, he and Steph get almost exactly the same grades, not counting gym, where Steph has all the physical advantages.

I decided a long time ago that Rat's general grouchiness is because he has to live with this everyday unfairness. In a weird way, though, he clings to Steph, as if he suspects that some of the best bits of himself might be trapped in her.

"I'm gonna bury Robin near the carport, close to his family," Rat informs us. "Either of you guys know any Bible prayers or poems?"

"I'll sing the National Anthem," Steph volunteers.

"I know a poem," I offer. "But it's not about a funeral or anything."

"Good enough so long as it rhymes." Rat examines the cross. "I think this'll hold."

"Dummy, should have used duct tape." Steph snatches the cross from him. "Yarn will e-rode in the rain."

"Not necessarily," I say quickly. "And the green color looks interesting."

Rat lifts his glasses and pinches his thumb and forefinger over the bridge of his nose. "Should've used the tape," he agrees. He's quiet for a second. I wonder if he's wondering why stuff that's always so obvious to Steph is so muddy to him.

Then I notice the open shoebox on his desk and the little gristle-gray lump inside it, resting on a bed of pink flowered toilet paper. Next to the lump and almost three times its size sits a large unripe mango. I move closer and bend down to get a better look. I thought the bat would be bigger somehow. His tiny closed face gives me goose pimples. Steph looks, too.

"Why are you burying Robin with that mango?" she asks.

"Custom," Rat answers confidently. "Down here, all the native people bury each other with food and valuables and stuff they might want to take to the other side."

"The other side of *what?*" Steph picks up the fruit. Rat frowns.

"The other side of *life*, obviously. *El otro lado de la vida*. Put that back." Steph pretends that she's going to bite into the mango, but then she replaces it.

"We're building the war fort today, remember," I tell Rat. "Are you helping?"

"I don't know that much about building." Rat stands up from his desk chair and stretches his knobby arms. "But I'll go with you. Dan says some kids from the other side are planning a surprise attack on our side." He picks up the lid of the shoebox from off the floor and closes Robin's casket. Steph starts jumping up and down on her tiptoes, squawking, "Jason McCullough? Is it a surprise attack from Jason McCullough?"

"What? Who's Jason McCullough?" Rat picks up the shoebox and hands me the cross. "Let's go."

The grave site is the corner of the Wagners' carport. I kneel with Steph and Rat at the tunnel-shaped opening he already dug in the shaded earth.

"But this is too narrow," Steph exclaims. "You'd have to push the shoebox in lengthways. I never saw a coffin go in like that."

"Neither have I," I admit.

"Well, excuse me, but how many funerals have either of you two seen?"

I stare at Robin's coffin and say nothing. Steph frowns, but sticks to her point.

"Robin and the mango will be all mushed down on the bottom if you put it in lengthways." Steph talks to him in a fake-nice, mostly annoyed voice, like a mean teacher. "And that's not how to respect the dead, Raymond, even if it's only a dead bat. Go get the shovel." Rat locks eyes with her, then jumps up and scurries back into the house. "*Loco* Rat," she sighs. "Can't see through a problem."

"Neither can a lot of people. Sometimes I can't."

"You," Steph scoffs. "You make up problems when they aren't even there."

Rat returns with a giant steel-tipped shovel and starts attacking the earth with grim energy. Dark orange dirt spews up into my eyes; I jump back. When the grave is ready we lower the shoebox carefully, like a casserole, into the earth and push and pat the loose soil back over it. I grind the cross into the ground and pack some more dirt up around its base.

"We will now stand for our National Anthem," Steph commands. She stretches to her feet, and motions us to copy her. "Oh say, can you see! By the dawn's early light!" Rat and I join in; our combined voices don't measure up to Steph's until the end of the song, after we've eased into it.

Then Rat says, "I want to say a few things. First, Robin, I'm sorry I didn't know you until I killed you by accident, since you seemed like a totally nice fruit bat." Steph glances up at me and rolls her eyes. "But since I did kill you, I'll never forget you. I will remember you for the rest of my life. And even though the encyclopedia said that fruit bats emit noise that is too high-pitched a frequency for the human ear to register — I'm pretty sure I heard your voice when I stepped on you, and I'm real sorry about that. Robin, rest in peace."

I try not to look at Steph, who's biting on her lips to keep from laughing. Instead I chew at the skin around my nails and look at Rat, who nods for me to begin.

"A poem about winter and summer," I announce, like I'm in front of a classroom. I know the poem by heart because it was Emily's and my favorite. She taught it to me and we used to say it together whenever it snowed in Rhode Island. I don't know why we did exactly, except that when snow is falling out of the sky it feels good to shout out something together to celebrate.

But then I start thinking about that broken, dead old bat in its toilet paper shoebox, in a cardboard coffin in the ground that we're going to leave all by itself forever. A sick cramp grabs hold of my stomach and then I can't get the poem past my lips. In my mind, I'm running over the paper-white lawn of our house, my mittened hand connected tight to Emily's, and we're singing the poem into the night while snowflakes sting and drip down our faces. But then, instead of snow, it's Robin who's falling, and his awful, high-frequency screaming is everywhere. The screaming gets louder and louder, filling my ears.

"Come on, Lane. It's hot." Steph's smirking eyes are on me.

A prickle of sweat breaks across my hairline. "A poem about winter and summer," I repeat. I look down at my sandals. I just know that Steph is rolling her eyes at Rat.

"Are you sure you don't you know any poems about dead things, Lane?" Rat asks me suddenly. "Like by those ladies who wrote stuff and then killed themselves?"

"Stop talking, you wink." Steph smoothes some damp vines of hair back from her sweaty face. "You're wrecking the funeral."

"Excuse me for living," Rat grumbles, but I can tell he feels like a doofus. "Sorry, Lane, go ahead."

I cross my arms, cupping my elbows with opposite hands, and breathe in deep through my nose and mouth so I can say it all out at once.

"In Winter I get up at night
And dress by yellow candlelight.
In summer, quite the other way,
I have to go to bed by day.

I have to go to bed and see
The birds still hopping on the tree.
Or hear the grown-up people's feet
Still going past me on the street."

It's not until the last line of the poem that I feel the spurt of pain through the insides of my arms and I realize that my fingernails have broken and dug through my own skin.

"Is it done?" Rat asks.

"The end." I nod. I drop my hands. I want to cry. Sometimes I think I miss Emily too much.

For a moment, we all stare at the puke yarn cross and the heap of mashed-down orange dirt.

"Let's eat," says Steph.

5

Mrs. Wagner prepares what my mom and dad call chemical food, but what Charlie and I always crusade for whenever we go along with one of them to the commissary. At each of our places is a peanut-butter-and-grape-jelly sandwich on chewy white Wonder bread cut into four triangles, barbecue potato sticks, and a package of Devil Dogs. Beside each plate is a cup of fruit cocktail, not the found-in-the-jungle-and-chunk-chopped-by-Marita kind, but the pastel-colored floating in heavy syrup good kind. We have our choice of Ovaltine or Tang.

"This looks great!" I say to Mrs. Wagner, who is hovering around the table, staring hard at the food like she forgot something.

"Do you want raviolis, too, sweetie?" she asks me. "Because it's easy enough to open a couple of cans . . ."

"We're okay, Mom." Rat flicks her away with his fingers and picks up a triangle of sandwich. Mrs. Wagner retreats through the swinging door, back into the kitchen.

"She's so annoying," Steph says to Rat and we begin feasting on the chemical lunch.

"I'd like some raviolis, though," comments Rat after a few minutes. "Hey, Mom!" Immediately Mrs. Wagner pops back in the dining room, like a genie. She waves a letter in one hand.

"Oh, you'll just never guess what's going on in the States on 'General Hospital'!" she breathes. "Aunt Patty —" she waves the letter. "Aunt Patty just filled me in on the whole scoop! I've got to call everyone!"

"I want raviolis," Rat whines. Mrs. Wagner blinks and stares at him for a moment, as if she's trying to refocus her excitement.

"Oh, right. Let me just heat some up for you and then I'll call the . . . I can't believe it! They eloped! I thought that might happen, I sure did, but to know . . . so, yes, sorry, Ray sugar, I'll be right in with the raviolis." She wanders back into the kitchen, her nose buried inside the letter.

"Mom says the first thing she's going to do when she gets back to the States is just sit down in front of the television for about two weeks straight and catch up on her soap operas," Steph says. Her mouth is full of cake. "I mean, it's bad enough that TV doesn't even come *on* here until three o'clock, but only one channel? With only Hee-Haw reruns and one soap per day? It hasn't even been fun staying home from school this whole week, from a TV point of view."

"How far behind is 'General Hospital' here, anyway?" I ask. My mom doesn't watch those kinds of shows, not in the States and not here, so it's nothing I ever really thought to miss.

"Like, two months. But my Aunt Patty always writes and updates her on it and on all the other shows, too. Mom's always the last to know, though, of her friends back in the States. Sort of sad for her." Steph shakes her head. "Poor Mom."

Poor Mom is right, I think. I never saw a mom treated as rudely by her family as Mrs. Wagner is — like a cross between a dumb housekeeper and an old dog. One of these days, I'd like Mrs. Wagner to show a little spirit — one day just yell, "Get your own dumb old raviolis, you lazy kids! I have work to do!" and slam a couple cans to the floor. Unfortunately, most of Mrs. Wagner's work is doing stuff like cooking up ravioli. I always have to remember not to let myself treat her like a housekeeper, too, although she pretty much invites it. Too much apologizing.

"Dan's here!" exclaims Rat. We follow his eyes out the dining room window to see Dan Fellicetti turning into the Wagners' walkway. Rat leaps up from the table, his knee jolting and spilling the pitcher of Tang. He ignores it though, and runs out the side door off the dining room.

"Mom!" shrills Steph. "Ray spilled!" Mrs. Wagner zips out of the kitchen holding a roll of paper towels and a damp sponge like she's an actress making her entrance on cue.

"It's no problem, I'll get it," she soothes. Outside the window, I can see Rat talking to Dan, who looks over to us and nods. Steph waves from the table. The two of them start walking back to the house.

"Dan, you hunk o' man! Hit me!" sings Steph, holding out the flat of her palm once Dan and Rat come into the dining room. I flush; how does Steph say things like that and not feel like a dork? It's always that way with Steph and me, though — she says the brave things, and then I get flooded with a rush of to-tal embarrassment for her.

Dan doesn't seem to care, though. He strikes her palm in a high-five. "Steph and Lane, the gruesome twosome. Lane, if you see Charlie today, will you ask him for my Steve Martin Wild and Crazy Guy T-shirt back? I know for a fact that he stole it from me the other day at Kobbe beach."

"I'll ask him." I know for a fact that Charlie stole it, too, along with Dan's New York Yankees hat. "I don't think he stole yours, though. I think the one he's been wearing is a different one."

"Aw, whatever. Just tell him to give it back, okay?"

"I'll tell him what you said," I grant, and put my glass of Ovaltine up against my mouth so I won't have to talk about it anymore.

Dan's eyes are cow brown and soft, but he also has a row of pointy teeth like a sawblade, so he has the right face for his personality, which I would call a mix of harmless-creepy. When Charlie stole that stuff from Dan, I didn't know why exactly, but I was sort of glad, although as his older sister I had to tell Charlie that he was basically on the road to becoming a kleptomaniac and a jailbird. That's the thing about Charlie, though. He'll actually *do* the crazy stuff I'd never even imagine attempting, but I usually appreciate the results.

Mrs. Wagner finishes wiping up the Tang and dashes back into the kitchen, returning with a big bowl of raviolis and another place setting for Dan. He quickly starts dishing up a helping without even a thank-you.

"Great raviolis," I tell her, to make up for Dan. Mrs. Wagner looks startled, then smoothes the smile back onto her mouth.

"Eat up, dear," she murmurs and then she's gone again.

"You'll see Charlie soon enough," Rat tells Dan,

"since he and Ted'll probably be picking us up to build the war fort."

"Good." Dan wipes some sauce from his face with the back of his hand and then smears it across his bare leg. "Charlie's a great kid, no questions there, but he can't just take other people's property." I know Dan's only saying Charlie's great because I'm around; a few months ago Steph told me that Dan said Charlie was a thug who'd probably beat up his own grandparents for five bucks. When I told Charlie what Dan said, he took it as a personal insult to Mina and Pops and he pantsed Dan at recess, then kept slamming him out in Dodge ball for a week. Dan definitely does not think of Charlie as a great kid. Dan's probably scared of Charlie. A lot of people are.

"Who is that kid you were talking about, Steph? Jason McIrish kid?" Rat asks her. "Maybe Dan knows him."

"Jason McCullough? He lives right on Sixth Street?"

"Hey, does living on Sixth Street make you on the other side or on our side?" I ask. Steph slaps her hand over her forehead.

"Lane! Duh! The other side, of course — and that's the totally most stupid question, it just shows how you don't even —"

"No, not so stupid," Rat doesn't look at me and two

spots of red appear on his cheeks. "Because Fort Bryan has an odd number of streets — eleven — some Sixth Street kids do go to our school."

"That's not true, Rat, no Sixth Street kids go to our school. Sixth Street is the other side. What about Heidi Carson from my Saturday gymnastics?" Steph looks mad. "She lives on Sixth and definitely doesn't go to our school, and won't even talk to me. Remember last week she even tried to steal —"

"Steph, if that's the girl I'm thinking of she's not talking to you because you called her a thumbsucker that day she —"

"I never heard of that kid, Jason McCullough," says Dan, very loud. "You sure he lives on Sixth Street? 'Cause I definitely would know the name McCullough from my lawn mowing."

"Yeah, he does." Steph sounds doubtful.

"Well, I don't know him." Dan lifts and drops his shoulders. "Maybe you're thinking of Kevin Mc-Cormick? Now *that* kid I know. His dad restores Corvettes." He sucks in another spoonful of raviolis. "These are Chef Boy-Ar-Dee, right?"

"I'm gonna get a Corvette when I turn sixteen." Rat holds out his hands like he's gripping a steering wheel and starts making squealing driving noises. As clear as if it's on a movie screen, this picture bursts into my mind's eye. I close my eyes and try to concentrate on the delicious cream filling of the Devil Dogs. I chew slow and slide the taste all over my mouth. *Go away*, my head whispers. My heart starts bumping along too fast, and the vision sweeps back through me.

"What kind do you want? Lane? Hey there, Lane." I open my eyes to see everyone frowning at me.

"Huh?"

"Car," huffs Dan impatiently. "What kind of car do you want?"

"Um, a coupe." Like Nancy Drew. In some books she drove a sporty roadster, but in other stories it was a coupe. The coupe sounds better — more expensive, although it's hard for me to picture one exactly.

"Not a Merc? Merc's are the best kind of car you can get," Rat says. *Calm down calm down*, whispers my head. *Stop thinking. Don't think.* I tuck my sweaty hands under my legs. *Please be normal. Don't do this, Lane*, I say to myself in my meanest inside voice.

"Besides," Steph is saying, "a coupe can be just any old type —"

"I need to use the phone for a sec," I say, pushing back my chair and standing. Dan, Rat, and Steph are quiet, staring at me. "Be right back." I smile like it's nothing.

I dash out to the living room and pick up the telephone receiver. I can't seem to find enough air to inhale.

"Hello?"

"Mom, it's Lane. Is Dad back?"

"Lane, don't do this to me. I mean it."

"Just tell me if he's safe."

On the other end of the phone, my mother sighs.

"Because I had a horrible flash of Dad and the jeep going over on its side. And there was fire everywhere." My fingers are shaking. I balance the phone between my chin and shoulder and squeeze my hands together. "Marita was in the jeep, too."

"He's back and he's safe, Lane. He's safe, Marita's safe. What else? Alexa is here, she's safe. I'm safe, but in a minute I'm driving to the grocery store and I might spontaneously combust on the way, or get hit on the head with a big can of tuna fish in aisle B."

"I had a bad spell." I speak low. "The fire — it seemed like it was happening for real." I drop down to my knees on the carpet.

"Lane, do you think you need to see Dr. Forrest again? I can make an appointment. Or what about the meditating? Why don't I sign you up for another session at the center? We could go together."

"No. I'm okay now." I breathe deep. I am silently repeating my word; I try to slow the chant to the pace of my heart.

"Lane?"

"What?"

"I'm going to make an appointment anyway."

"I won't go. I'm okay now. Marita's there, too?"

"She's here, he's here. Everyone's here, everyone's safe."

"Okay, then." I say quietly. My heart is dropping back down to its normal tap. "Oh, and Mom, Dad invited" — I cup my hand over the receiver — "Army People to the party. I didn't tell him in time."

"He told me. Just the Wagners, though, right?"

"I think so," I whisper. "I'm sorry."

"It's okay. If too many others come, we'll just make them sit on the porch and we won't feed them." She laughs, mostly to get me to laugh, but I don't. "You and Charlie be home by six for dinner. Daddy and I have to go to Major Gregory's change of command at the Officer's Club, but we'll be back by seven-thirty, eight. Okay?"

"Yep."

"And stop worrying."

"Yep." I hang up. The Wagners' blue ocean carpet looks so restful. I lie down on the carpet and close my eyes. My body feels limp, like those papery-winged brown moths that get trapped inside our house. Whenever I see them, dead in Marita's dustpan, I always try to think how it served the moth right for heading like a kamikaze pilot right into our burning hot lightbulbs. Still, those dumb moths make me sad, especially when Marita sweeps them off to their garbage can graves. What a strange place to die and be buried, in a place that doesn't have anything to do with how you lived. Even if you are just a moth, it's a shame.

From far away I think I hear Charlie's voice. He and Ted must have arrived already. Maybe they'll all just go along and build the war fort without me. Then I could sleep for a while. I can hear them talking and laughing. Soon their voices are only little hooks of noise that catch me from drowning into sleep.

"Hey, Sleeping Ugly, are you sick?" Charlie's voice jerks my eyes open.

"I didn't hear you come in."

"Why are you lying down on the rug? Everyone's heading out." He crouches beside me. "Let's go."

"Mom thinks I should see Dr. Forrest again."

"Old Forehead? What for?"

"For my worrying. What do you think?"

"How do I know? It's not like it's the job of my life to understand about *you*, Lane," Charlie says impatiently.

"Should I go back to Dr. Forrest, though?"

"I'd rather be crazy all day long than listen to that lady again." He flattens his hair back from his forehead and in a froggy voice says, "Hello, I'm Dr. Forehead. What are you problems? My problem is that

I'm a big, boring pumpkin-head since all I do is listen to other people's problems."

I smile and Charlie punches my arm, not quite hard enough to hurt. "Get up. Everyone's waiting. If you act normal for a few days, we can all forget about it."

6

While Mrs. Wagner fidgets and twitches, but dares not say a word, Dan, Steph, Rat, and I pile into the flatbed of Ted's old truck. Bundles of rough yellow wooden planks, tied and stacked, take up most of the room. Charlie's up front, but he has to hold the hand-saw and Ted's toolbox on his lap. Ted refuses to let the toolbox out of his sight, for even a second, al-though the only one who'd ever think of stealing it is Charlie.

We each slurp a Popsicle from the box Mrs. Wag-ner passed around after lunch. Mine is grape. Purple juice rolls down my wrist faster than I can lick it away and my fingers are stained and sticky. Steph and Rat both picked lime and their lips are smeared green.

"All on?" Ted shouts. He starts the ignition.

"Are you kids safe?" Mrs. Wagner finally peeps. "I mean, isn't this a little dangerous, with everyone in the back and no seatbelts?" Steph and Rat look straight ahead, like they don't have any connection to this weird lady who decided to come out of her house and ask us questions.

"Ted's a good driver," I say. I feel like I *have* to say something. "And we're just going over to Third Street."

"You should stop by and pick up Dana Franken, then. Her family lives on First Street, I think, and she seems like a nice girl."

I can't answer because the truck lurches away from her, kicking up a cloud of dust.

"Did you hear her say that?" Steph bares her teeth and opens her eyes wide like Orphan Annie. "Frankenstein's daughter? So we could talk about what — Ozzy Osbourne and ACDC? And it's not even on the way. Why's Mom just so totally, incredibly winky?"

"Don't worry about it, Steph." Rat scratches his chin. "Hey, you know, maybe we should cruise over to the other side and check out the other fort."

"Good plan." Dan leans into the rear view window and signals.

"What?" shouts Ted over his shoulder. He slows down the truck.

"Check out the other side first," Dan yells. "The competition, right?"

"Done." Ted yells back. "But first we gotta swing around to Fifth Street and get Mary Jane Harris." I snake my eyes a fraction over to my right to catch Steph's reaction. She'd been slouched, mosquito-gnawed legs splayed out in front of her and arms spread-eagled over the sides of the truck, but at the mention of Mary Jane Harris's name she yanks herself up so that her spine is rifle straight.

"I don't think so!" she brays. "I do not think so!"

"Let it go," Rat tells her. "Forget about it."

"I don't think so!" Steph tries to stand and manages a wobbling stoop. She begins pounding her fist on the roof of the truck on the driver's side. Ted swerves off to the shoulder of the road and brakes; we all hang on to the walls of the truck at the sudden motion. Ted leaps out and looks up at Steph, who's now planted in the center of the truck. Green-mouthed, hands clamped on her hips and feet locked a shoulder's width apart, she looks like a mule or a skinny version of Wonder Woman.

"She comes, I go." Steph rubs the side of her nose and flicks the sweat off her fingers.

"She comes. I invited her yesterday at Kobbe and she called me this morning," Ted answers flatly.

"Then I go."

"What's your problem, Steph?"

"Unless she admits she never jumped off the Miraflores water tower." Steph holds up one finger. "I know for a fact she didn't and for a month she's told everyone she did, which makes her a liar, because her initials aren't up there. I should know because mine are up since I'm the only girl I know who ever jumped! Ever!"

"Here we go again." Rat snaps his Popsicle stick in half and begins tapping them on his knee in a drumbeat. "Day-oh!" He sways his head and sings in reggae rhythm, "Day-light come and Steph never for-get."

"Shut up, Rat," Steph snaps.

"Steph, no one cares about this except you," Ted sighs.

"You wouldn't say that if Mary Jane was a guy. You'd care — you'd make him do a do-over."

Ted pauses, and I can tell he can't figure out if he agrees with her on this point or not. "Let's just go by her house and see what she says." He pulls off his shirt and ties it like a bandanna over his head. "Maybe ask her for a do-over and see what happens, okay?"

"Okay." Steph looks smug. They exchange a nod of truce and Ted climbs back in the truck. Steph slouches back and closes her eyes, her chin dropped down to her chest. Her expression reminds me of a boxer during a time-out.

"This should be interesting." I try for a careless laugh and a toss of my hair, like Nancy Drew. Except that Nancy Drew's hair is titian-colored, which I looked up and it's just a complicated, pretty way of saying red. I can't think of a pretty way of saying dark brown. Dead grass, dirt, moths, meatloaf . . . only ugly, boring things are dark brown.

"Hey, you don't think Mary Jane Harris actually jumped, do you?" Steph's eyes crack open to glare at me.

"Well, if she was at the tower, someone had to take her there, right? It's not like she rowed herself out there all alone. So who are her witnesses?"

"She says it was her hicksville cousins visiting from the States." Steph leans out of the truck and shoots a lime-green wad of spit into the road. "That's convenient, huh?"

"We'll hear the story soon enough," Rat grumbles. "Like we haven't heard it a hundred times before already."

"It ain't fair, though." Steph never says "ain't" unless she's really peeved about something. She flutter-kicks her heels, and the metal floor sounds like a kettle-drum beneath us. "I one hundred percent know that she didn't jump. I just *know*, because she got a lot of facts wrong when I quizzed her about exactly how it feels to fall down from so high and plus she didn't put in her initials before she went. I don't see why Ted invited her to come along with us, anyway. It's not like she's in our usual group. Why couldn't he have asked Chris Lorno or Tim Polanski? Mary Jane Harris! That girl's such a wink! She gives girls a bad name!"

"Calm down there, Steph." Rat reaches over and pinches the toe of her sneaker. "You act like jumping off the top of the Miraflores tower is the biggest thing in the world."

Steph quiets down but I can almost hear what she's thinking — that Rat wouldn't know since he's too chicken to jump. I am, too.

Showing some loyalty to Steph's side of the story, Ted rudely beeps the horn when we pull up to Mary Jane's house instead of getting out and walking to the door the way he usually does. Mary Jane sweeps out immediately, swinging her ugly white fishnet purse that she carries everywhere and wearing a pair of purple-rimmed sunglasses. Steph huffs, "What're those stupid glasses —" but Rat smacks Steph quick on the shin to interrupt her before Mary Jane can hear.

"How do, all?" Mary Jane slurs in her funny Southern accent, hoisting herself up into the flatbed. She thumps the side of the truck, so Ted knows to push off, but it stays stopped. We all mumble hellos; everyone's nervous, waiting for Steph's attack. She doesn't disappoint us.

"Look, M.J.," she starts off immediately. "We're all having a problem with this supposed, so-called jump you made off the Miraflores tower last month, which no one saw and no initials to prove it." Steph's saying "we" makes me look down and start examining my fingernails.

"My cousins seen. They seen when they come down to visit, but all of 'em're home, now." Mary Jane talks like she's stumbling for the right words. "Y'all know they went back to Roybrush, to Georgia."

"Ain't good enough." Steph stretches out her bony arms behind her and then lets her neck drop back into the sling she's made from her interlocked fingers. She draws her elbows together in front of her face. Now no one can see her lips talk. "I am officially challenging you to a do-over, Mary Jane Harris. Today if possible. So that none of us has any doubts."

Up in the driver seats, the backs of Ted and Charlie's heads are still, listening. The purple-rimmed glasses shield most of Mary Jane's expression and she doesn't speak for a while. Dan leans out the side of the truck and hucks a glob of grape spit. I copy him, watching it sizzle to nothing on the black road. Rat coughs into his hand. The sun feels like it's broiling up my sweat before it has a chance to cool me down, and it hurts when I unstick my fricasseed legs from the floor of the truck.

"Look here," Mary Jane finally says. "I done it before, I do it again. Anytime. Y'all can be witnessers."

"Fine," Steph says. "Right." She looks a little confused. I bet she was hoping for a crybaby breakdown and confession.

Ted pulls away from the curb. No one speaks. Mary Jane rummages in her big ugly pocketbook and extracts a tube of Bonnie Bell spearmint lipgloss, and she begins to slather it over her lips. I breathe the layered smell of mint and lumber and close my eyes against the tension of Steph's clamped face.

We turn off Fifth Street and onto Main Road, which runs clear from the front gate of Fort Bryan all the way to the back entrance. Every public building on base is located just off Main Road, all in sight. We pass the squat commissary and the red-tile roofed post office, the box-shaped church, and the compact shopping complex where a few stores offer a limited selection of shoes or bedsheets or lamps. Most of what Mom buys comes from catalogs from the States or downtown, off-base. We pass the Rec Center, where you can go bowling or take karate classes, the movie theater with only one screening room, and over the hill, all by itself, the gym where everyone plays racquetball. There are only two courts and you have to call to reserve a spot almost a week in advance. Charlie and I love to play racquetball, even though he usually wins, and we always fight over who gets the blue-grip racquet.

Suddenly Charlie twists around from the front and yells, "We should grab one so I can crush you again."

"I'll call when we get home," I say.

"What are you guys talking about?" Dan stares at me with a frown between his eyes. "I hate it when you both do that weird mind-reading stuff. Steph and Rat are *twins*, and they never do that."

"Speaking of getting crushed," Steph says, her eyes thoughtful in the distance. "We need to get some weapons for our fort. Those kids from the other side mean business."

"Yeah." Everyone agrees in grave voices — even me, although I wonder if everyone's clear on what "mean business" really means. In fact, even though I'd never really admit it to Steph or Charlie, or even Ted, I'm not sure why we fight against the other side kids at all, except that we don't know them because they don't go to our school.

We're winding along past Ninth Street when Charlie calls out, "Where's their fort, anyway?"

"Behind Tenth," Rat shouts back. "All the way in back of the basketball courts."

By the time we climb down from the truck, I'm excited to see the other side's fort for myself. Tenth Street is long and mostly uphill, and we make a straggly path up to a building stamped #8BQ; a plain gray block divided by cookie-cutter lines of curtain-less windows. Dan says it's where unmarried soldiers live and that BQ stands for Bachelors' Quarters. The basketball court lies behind it. It's just a sunken rect-angle of poured concrete, with stairs leading down — built like a swimming pool that's all shallow end. Weeds spring up in the loose chinks, and a deflated basketball is slumped in the corner.

The kids from the other side have built their fort in the far backyard of the BQ. We spot the fort immedi-ately; it looks like Mina and Pop's old outhouse, only it's built against a thick-trunked tree. I can just see the bicycle chain and lock twisted tight around the door. But what I don't see is what Charlie spies immediately.

"Kid," he hisses.

We stop in our tracks. It's then that I notice the skinny legs, attached to a pair of blue sneakers, dan-gling from the tree.

7

The rest of the body's invisible, lost in a rubbery leaf awning. We don't know if the kid sees us so we approach carefully. Charlie glances at me with that weird, blank expression he always gets when he's in the middle of a situation that he can't predict. I don't even swallow; water gathers slowly in my mouth as we shove through the ragged weed grass. I do notice that Steph takes the opportunity to catch hold of Ted's wrist, but he doesn't seem to care.

"Hey, kid!" Charlie shouts. Rat and I exchange an anxious look. I hope he's thinking what I'm thinking, that more kids might be hidden inside the tree. The tree crackles and the legs draw up and disappear inside it.

"What are you? Scaredy-cat? Cats climb trees but they can't get down!" Charlie's voice picks up confidence. He's proud of his cat comparison. "Here, kitty

kitty kitty!" Charlie's now leading us all by a few paces. He looks over his shoulder and motions to us. "Come on, guys. There's seven of us and one of him. Let's take him!" He breaks for the tree.

"Wait, Charlie. Hang on a second!" My own voice strains my throat. "Maybe there's more kids, okay, so let's just see —" But then Dan tears away, too, speeding after Charlie. They reach the tree together. Charlie points up into the leaves; then Dan crouches and makes a stirrup with his hands to give Charlie a leg-up.

"Ooh, they-all're just plumb *loco*!" Mary Jane adjusts her purple sunglasses with her matching grape-painted nails. "It's kinda like a war!"

"Shut up, Mary Jane," murmurs Steph. "It *is* a war."

Charlie swings up from Dan's handmade rung to grab the lowest branch of the tree. I watch as he squirms, legs kicking at the air, working to thrust his weight onto the branch.

"Here kitty, kitty," he grunts. Ted snickers. Charlie makes a final heave up to try beaching his stomach on the branch, but he never gets that far. With a surprised yelp of pain, Charlie suddenly lets go of the tree limb and falls to a thud on the dirt. He doesn't move. I start running.

"Charlie!" I cry out to him. "Charlie, I'm coming!"

I drop down to all fours on the dirt beside him.

Dan's scowling up into the tree. Charlie moans and slowly rolls over on his side, his knees bent up under his chin like a crushed mosquito.

"That kid stepped on my hands," he wheezes. "Wind's knocked out of me! Ah, Jeez — my stomach!" But it's Charlie's knuckles that look painful and disgusting, all shredded, ripped, and bloody skin.

An angry cry from Dan distracts my attention; I turn to see him gripping his head with both hands.

"Rocks!" he yelps. "Damn kid just hit me with a rock!" It takes me a second to understand what Dan means, but not before something knocks against the back of my head. For a split second I'm numb, and then pain shoots from the base of my skull and spreads down through me like a stain. Charlie's already back on his feet, bellowing. He rubs his knuckles on the sides of his shorts, leaving dirty marks of blood smudged against the khaki.

"You stupid kid! There's seven of us and one of you, you freak kid!"

A large green rock whistles from the tree, grazing Charlie's shoulder. I crane my neck to get a better look and realize it's not a rock; it's a green mango.

"Get to the side, over to the side!" Ted is yelling, has been yelling. He waves us in with his arms. He and the others stand in a frozen knot, out of range. Mangoes now are spitting from the tree in rapid fire.

One thuds hard on my toes; I stagger to my feet and start moving away from the tree fast.

Idiot that he is, Charlie charges to the base of the tree and starts trying to shinny up its trunk.

"That's no mango tree either," Dan yells, jumping up and down. "They must have brought some supplies up there. Charlie, don't be dumb. We'll get 'em later."

"Get back, Charlie!" I call out. "We'll all come back later!"

"With helmets!" Steph adds. She looks at me. "That kid might have worse than mangoes up there," she confides. "He could have a whole, you know, arsenal — BB-guns, machetes, blinding sand, you name it."

"What's blinding sand?" I ask. I flinch, watching the mangoes beat like green hailstones against Charlie's back and shoulders. Both his hands are clamped over his head and I feel slightly nauseated as I watch a mango smack against his bloody fingers.

"You don't want to know. It's like getting pepper in your eye, and then you're permanently blinded," Steph tells me. "For life."

I prod Ted in the shoulder.

"Do something. Make Charlie get back."

"What can I do? Move to the side, Charlie," he

shouts so loud that I can see veins tighten in his neck. "You're acting like a stupid little kid."

Watching Charlie not listening to us reminds me of this other time, after the accident, when Charlie and I were both in the hospital, placed in the same room in beds side by side because the doctors thought it would be easier for us that way. So much of him was messed up, not just his leg and his shoulder, but in his head he wasn't exactly right either. Every morning Charlie would thump out of bed and pull back the divider that was rigged up like a shower curtain in the middle of our room. I'd hear the slither of the metal rings push back, and I'd open my eyes to see him standing next to my bed in his green hospital nightshirt.

"I'm going to look for her again. Are you coming to help?"

"You can't just leave your room, Charlie. It's a *hospital*," I always said.

"Are you coming to help?"

"You can't just leave."

"Are you coming to help?" Back and forth our words would slide, until he gave up and left without me. I would be by myself for a few minutes, and then I'd hear the nurses' voices; caught by surprise, yelling at him, delivering him back into our room. Those moments when Charlie was gone made me feel nervous and lonely, but when they'd bring him back I always felt too sorry for him to look at him.

I feel the same way now.

"Do something, Ted," I say again.

"Charlie, you cretin, report back here double time!" he shouts.

Charlie finally must register Ted's voice because he looks up.

"We can take him, you and me, Ted," he calls frantically. A mango bounces solidly off his shoulder and lands by his feet. Charlie winces and touches his hand to the target.

"Yeah, but not now. Forget about it for now."

Charlie holds Ted in his eyes for a long second; then his eyes pin back on the tree. He starts circling the tree suspiciously like a bear who can't climb but knows his dinner's up there somewhere.

"Forget about it," Ted repeats.

"Come on, Charlie," Dan adds, with an exasperated look at Ted. "Kid's a serious head case," he mumbles.

Charlie finally starts backing away from the tree in slow, careful steps, like he thinks the kid might just leap out of the tree. But the tree is silent and the mango missiles stop.

"Let's go," he mutters detachedly, as he joins us. "Let's just get out of here. I'll come back."

"You and me," Ted answers. "Tomorrow, how about?"

"Yeah."

Our defeat hurts Charlie most. Even I, rubbing the back of my head in search of blood (there's none), don't care so much about revenge. But Charlie's always distracted by new battles, and knowing he's losing never makes him think of stopping. I understand that much about Charlie, anyway. Not like it really matters; a person can't fix Charlie just by explaining him.

"Ted, you still got your first aid kit in the truck?" I ask.

"Yeah. Let's clean you up, Charleston. That's your real name, right, Charleston? Isn't that what the Duchess named you?" Ted elbows Charlie in the ribs.

"Shut up, Ted." Charlie's mouth twists up in a kind of smile. "It's just Charles, you Zone-iguana. Charleston — what am I, on 'General Hospital'?"

"There's a Port Charles on 'General Hospital'," Mary Jane informs us. "Does your mama lookit 'General Hospital'?" We are pushing back through the weeds to the truck. None of us looks over our shoulders to the fort and the enemy hidden in the tree.

"Yeah, maybe you were named for Port Charles," Steph's face brightens. "My middle name's Amber, named after a royal lady from this book my mom read.

Real royalty, I mean, not like in some fake romance story."

"I was named for my grandfather, who fought in World War II. Commanding Officer Charles Garfield Fogarty," Charlie says proudly. "Not for 'General Hospital,' Steph, you retard."

"I wonder," Steph muses. "That kid in the tree might have been Jason McCullough. In fact, I bet it was."

"Steph, you've got zero idea what you're talking about," Ted snaps.

Steph looks hurt, but of course she keeps at it. "How do you know, Zonie? I think I recognized those blue sneakers from soccer camp. It's not like you know what he looks like."

"It's not like blue sneakers prove that it's Jason McCullough."

"It's not like they don't."

"Whatever." Ted looks at Steph in such a way that she decides not to push it. We then walk without talking the rest of the way to the truck.

8

Our own fort site lies between Third and Fourth
Streets, on an inclined sweep of field. Ted had
checked it out before and picked it for its privacy.
Since the location's close to a swampland near the
edge of the jungle, the houses are built far away and
the land is too soggy, even for military drills. The
grass is kept short as a crew cut, though, because the
field technically is Bravo Company property. That, at
least, is what Ted says. Ted always seems to know
more army facts than anyone else. He's seen lots of
families come and go, and he's combed the bases his
whole life. He can tell me the names of four families
who lived in our house before it got stamped #4J, LT.
COL. BECK.

We post sticks at the four corners of the fort, which
we decide to build in the shade of a lanky tree — way
too puny for us to use as a climbing hideout plus

arsenal. Still, it'll give our fort some protection from the sun.

Ted ticks off on his fingers who's responsible for what. Charlie and Dan and he will nail the framework together, Steph and Rat can start shaping the door, and Mary Jane and I will dig out all the weeds and rocks and other junk that's embedded in what will be our floor space.

We all unload the wooden planks from the truck, making a few trips apiece. As Steph and Charlie tug a heavy board from the flatbed, she peers over at Charlie's skin-grated fingers.

"He really got you bad,"

"It doesn't hurt, though. Not like my stomach when I hit the ground."

"Jason McCullough's a wild kid. He's so wild that his dad ties him up outside on a leash like a dog to punish him. Crazy, most likely," Steph says. Her voice seems to me to be a little bit gleeful. She sure likes that tied-up dog story.

"Hey, Charlie, that reminds me." Dan sits on the edge of the truck, fishing around for tools in Ted's toolbox. "Last week at the beach, I think you must've accidentally picked up my Steve Martin T-shirt, the one where he's holding the balloons and it says 'Wild and Crazy Guy' underneath. I think I saw you wearing it the other day when you were out bike riding." Dan doesn't look at Charlie while he talks. He lifts out different sized screwdrivers from Ted's tool box and compares them carefully.

"Maybe I have it," Charlie responds indifferently. "But if I do, it's in the wash."

"Whenever you can get it back to me, I kind of want it." Dan keeps his eyes harmless as a puppy, but now he looks up directly at Charlie, who's scaling a piece of wood with Ted's measuring tape.

"If you're so positive it's yours, what T-shirt have you got I might like?" Charlie asks, which is his way of saying he'll exchange the Steve Martin shirt for something else of Dan's. It's not exactly a fair trade, except in a Charlie way. Dan knows by now that whatever string he tries to pull, the same tangle of Charlie-logic will fall down on his head. The trick is figuring out how to pull down what you want without yanking Charlie into a fight you know you'll lose.

"I'll check around," Dan says casually. He smiles to himself, so I guess he feels pretty good about the conversation and the swap, and he should. On a bad day Charlie would have denied taking anything.

We work without speaking, except to ask Ted what goes where and how to do certain things. The kid in the tree stole our good mood, but gave us a purpose.

After a while, the space between my shoulder blades starts aching. Between us, Mary Jane and I have heaped up a pretty big pile of crumbly-rooted weeds, and my hands are sore from the effort.

"I need a break," I tell her. Mary Jane nods.

"I need water," she chuffs. Ted looks up from his hammering.

"What a couple of lightweights," he snorts. "I'm glad you're not on my payroll."

"Yeah, come on, you two," Steph agrees. "Get back to it." I know she's just talking so that Ted notices she hasn't stopped working.

Dan looks up from his digging. Sweat has separated his hair into dark bands. "Now I know how bad it must have been to dig the Canal," he half-jokes. "Phew — the ground is tough to break through."

"Aw, you don't have it near as bad as those poor guys who dug the Canal," Ted says. "People *died* trying to get that thing finished."

"Wasn't it a lot of Korean people?" Mary Jane asks. "That's what my dad told me anyway."

"A lot of Chinese, not Korean, people, a lot of locals, some Americans; it was a lot of people came down who'd never been here before in their lives. Laborers, man. Serious raw deal, trying to build the Canal." Ted stops hammering and unscrews the lid from his canteen, takes a long swallow of water and then passes it to Mary Jane. "Tons of people got sick and died from all the stuff they weren't . . . prepared for? What's the word I'm looking for, Lane-brain?"

"Immune?"

Ted snaps his fingers and points at me like a game show host. "Immune, right! They weren't immune. So they got all these really bad diseases and infections like malaria and yellow fever and dysentery."

Mary Jane makes a shuddering sound and passes the canteen to me. I take a drink; the water tastes like warm pennies. I recap the bottle and toss it over to Steph.

"Yellow fever's that disease where you can't digest anything and so you starve to death, right?" Dan asks.

"Something like that. I don't really know, but the reason they called it yellow fever was because of the Chinese people being yellow-skinned," Ted says.

"No, the reason they called it yellow fever was because they thought the sickness came from the sun," I tell him. "I read that last year in social studies or somewhere."

"Both you guys are wrong. Yellow is what you call someone if they're a coward." Charlie sighs, as if he's bored having to explain something so obvious. "Cowboys used to say like — you're yellow, and then that was a total insult. So yellow fever is, uh — different from regular fever, because you know you're going to die, and so you're really scared, like a coward. Yellow fever — see?"

We're all quiet a moment, turning over this strange new information, and then Charlie adds, "The only thing is, though, I know if I had yellow fever, I would probably be pretty scared to die, but I'm no coward." A vicious expression fixes on his face, like he's daring anyone to call him a coward. "Pass me the water, too."

"Coward fever?" Rat says, looking at Steph. "I never heard that." Steph nods like she heard of it.

"Well, there's a lot of kind of yellowish-skinned Chinese still living here, and they're descendants of the Canal diggers." Ted hangs on to his point.

"Chinese people here don't have pure yellow skin." Rat shakes his head. "It's more of a goldish-brown colored."

"I think Lane's right, anyway." Mary Jane nods. "Once I got sunburned real bad? And all these hives and bumps were just *trifling* my whole entire skin? And Doc Perkins says, better get this gal some kammymeal lotion, for this here could turn into a bad spell of sun-yellow fever!"

Steph gives Mary Jane the slit-eye. I can tell that she's fueling up for another attack on Mary Jane's inability to tell the truth.

"Hey, what was that song Mrs. Ellerson taught us about the mule and the canal last year in music?" I ask

Steph. "Do you remember?" Steph doesn't even see me; she won't look away from Mary Jane.

"Mary Jane Harris," she fumes. "You did not once ever get yellow fever, okay? Because before you came down here you got a bunch of shots, remember? And one of them, if you recall, was called a yellow-fever shot? And no — I repeat no — doctor's going to look at a little bit of sun poisoning and be dumb enough to think it's a symptom of yellow fever, unless he happens to be a cowpoke relative of yours or something. You'll say anything for attention, I swear." Steph's eyes are hard as bullets.

"I know what song you're talking about." Rat turns to me. " 'Erie Canal,' it's called. About the mule." Softly, he starts to sing, "I got a mule, her name is Sal —"

"Fifteen miles on the Erie Canal." I join in. My voice sounds too high pitched and girly, which is sort of embarrassing. "She's a good old worker and a good old pal."

"Fifteen miles on the Erie Canal!" Charlie bawls, totally off-key but very confident.

"Just one more stop and back we'll go, through the rain and sleet and snow! 'Cause we know every inch of the way, from Al-ban-ee to the Buh-fu-lo — Oh!" Soon everyone's singing, except Ted, who didn't learn "Erie Canal" in *Escuela Balboa*. We sing-shout it through a couple times, then Rat starts off with "Don Gato," another music class song, and this time Ted knows it.

I pull up more weeds, finding fresh energy with the singing. It's rewarding, anyway, tugging at a weed until I feel its witch-fingered roots detangling from the dirt. I keep count of how many Mary Jane tosses in the pile so that I always stay one or two weeds ahead of her. Little private games like that always keep me working longer and faster than normal.

"The fort's looking good!" Dan exclaims. "Check it out." He stands and stumbles backward a little from where he'd been hammering. I stand up, too, stretching out the crick in my back. It looks better than good; I can see the beginnings of a real war fort: two solid walls of rough-cut wood sunk tight into the ground over the skeleton box Ted, Dan, and Charlie had constructed. Mary Jane's and my work has cleared the ground to a floor of solid dirt. Steph's and Rat's plywood door is sanded and hinged, ready to slot into place once the third side of the fort is put up.

Ted looks up. "Time to go swimming."

"I could use the bath," Dan announces. "I stink."

"So let's get over to Miraflores." Ted starts replacing scattered tools and nails into his toolbox. "Before it rains, right?" He pretends to pop Steph on the head with his hammer.

"I'm ready. Pack up and ship out!" Steph's voice is hard and fast enough to make us all remember why she wants to get going.

I check Mary Jane for signs of nervousness. She's kneeling on our new fort floor, spitting into her hands and scrubbing them together to wash off the grass and dirt stains, but doesn't look scared about the tower or her jump. I bet she's plotting her escape. That would be a pretty interesting, Nancy Drewish thing to do. Except that Nancy would already have jumped off the tower bravely and afterward laughed while shaking out her dampened curls.

"Creo que va a llover." Ted speaks to the sky. *"Tengo mucho calor y estoy sudando."*

"Huh?" Steph laughs and blinks her eyes at him. "Translation, please."

"Just that I wish it'd rain — I'm hot and bothered." He ruffles his hair so that it stands up in spikes.

Ted and his parents talk a lot in Spanish — they're not like a lot of other Zonians, who only speak Spanish if they absolutely have to, and then use a flat American accent. That kind of Spanish sounds strange, though, like bad acting in a dubbed movie. It's almost as if the Zonians are trying to insult the words while they speak them. Ted says the dialect makes Zonians feel more separate from the locals, more like Americans.

"Ted Tie, Touch and Die!" Steph tries to give herself a man voice. She picks up Ted's toolbox. "Ted, does that mean if I touch you, I'll die?"

"Only from ecstasy at my physique." Ted flexes an arm, and then seizes his toolbox from her.

"Oh right." Steph laughs and draws her own bony self up to full height.

Sometimes, especially when they aren't arguing, the combination of Ted and Steph needles me. I'm always sort of half-waiting for the day those two decide they don't like the rest of us. I could see Steph counting us off with her fingers — *Dan's too weak, Charlie's too unstable, Lane's too quiet, and Mary Jane's too girly. Rat can be slow* ... Although Steph would never ever completely turn against Rat, she's quick to dismiss him with her mean eyes and her teacher-talk.

As we walk back to the truck, loaded like pack mules with scrap wood and tools, Mary Jane is suddenly at my elbow.

"Lane, I was fixing to tell you something." Her voice is secretive and I turn to look at her. She's pushed her sunglasses to the top of her head and finally I can see her face, pale and easy to read.

"You never jumped, right?" I say.

"No."

"That's too bad."

"Think she'd push me off?" Mary Jane's forehead puckers slightly as she frowns.

"No way." I watch Steph striding ahead, talking casually to Ted and Rat in a way that nevertheless looks like she's giving orders. "But if I were you, I'd rather jump and hurt myself than not jump and —"

"Yeah, I know. Have Steph on my back until we relocate." Mary Jane cuts me off. "Don't go gabbing about it to anyone, okay?"

"I wouldn't."

She brushes past me then, rushing to the front of the line as if suddenly she's impatient to get the jump over and done with.

9

Ted has the right identification to use the dock and the Canal patrol skiff because of his dad. During school breaks, Ted himself sometimes works as a line handler for the ships. Today, he parks the truck on the bank of the Miraflores lock and pays an old local man working on the dock fifty cents to watch over it.

We take the boat to get to the tower. The skiff has a low-power outboard motor, and there are so many of us crammed in together that I worry through the whole ride that we will sink. It doesn't help that as soon as we move far enough away from the dock, Charlie launches into a long story about alligators. He talks on about how they swim down from Florida to live in the locks and once they snap you up, they'll drag you down and bury you in mud flats for days before eating you. "So you're nice and soft and rotten to sink their teeth into," he finishes, looking at me.

"Whatever, Charlie. No alligators live here."

"Rotting, decomposing flesh."

"If you don't shut up I'm going to push you overboard." I shove away from him and stare down at the brown, murky image of myself that trembles on the surface of the water. Silent orange fish dart beneath my face; they flicker and are gone like candle flames. Then the water turns black; I look up into the sky and for the first time notice that clouds have gathered and are covering the sun. It seems like it happened in an instant.

"You were right," I say to Ted. "About the rain."

"We better jump quick is all I'm thinking," he yawns. "Lightning. Of course, we could always sacrifice Charlie to the Lightning Gods and then maybe it won't rain so hard. Tie him to the top of the tower, sling a shell necklace around his neck . . ."

"Please feel free to shut up anytime, Ted." Charlie beats on his chest with his fists. "I'm too tough to sacrifice."

"It'd be nobler than a lot of other ways you might meet your maker, Charlie. Lightning Gods — gotta love 'em." Ted scans the water. "Land-ho! I see the Eiffel tower."

The Miraflores water tower is a tall skinny rusty

iron scaffolding that stretches up about twenty-five feet out of the river. We call it the water tower because that's all we know about how to describe it, although Ted once said it's a watermark to let ship captains know how deep the Canal is in this part of the lock. I don't know if that's truth or Zonie-truth. Zonies like to make up stuff about the Canal and the Zone and the locals, hoping military people accept it as God's truth. They know that no matter how dumb it is, we'll most probably believe it, since we wouldn't know any different.

Ted ropes the skiff to one of the scaffold legs and cuts the engine. We all tip off the boat, falling into the water, shoes and all, and then we scale the iron rungs of the tower up to the halfway ledge, which is the only part wide enough to hold all of us comfortably at once.

There's enough room to stretch out and relax. The water is patterned with the reflection of shifting clouds. I can stare over the entire width of the lock to the messy snarl of jungle that always borders the horizon. I sit and wrap my arms tight around myself. Everyone else is talking, but I let their voices blend over me, turning into one faded color. For a minute I feel like I'm part of a picture that's existed millions of years before me, and it's weird to think it'll just keep being here after I am gone.

I hook my legs over the grilled ledge of the tower

and lie back, my hands crossed underneath my head. Mary Jane lies down next to me while Rat lies on the other side, the opposite way. His head almost touches mine. I hear the others clank up the rungs on their way to the very top, to the jump point.

"You coming, Mary Jane?" shouts Steph from above. She has climbed past the halfway ledge to a higher point on the tower. Her voice bubbles with fake sweetness. "We're all doing the second highest jump for practice before we do the highest."

"I'm fixing on one jump," Mary Jane shouts up. She makes her words strong and loud. "So y'all can practice all you need without me."

"Suit yourself," answers Steph. "Dan says if you do the highest jump, he will too. *He* admits he never did the biggie before."

"We'll go together. Suicide pact," shouts Dan's voice.

"Sure thing," Mary Jane sings out. She sighs.

"Don't think about it before and it won't seem so bad when it happens," I say to reassure her.

"Tell me one of your stories, Lane." she says. "Take my mind off."

"Did I ever tell you about the time Charlie and I cleaned the kitchen?" I ask. Mary Jane shakes her head no.

"Thing was, we didn't have to clean it but Emily —

I've told you about her, she was our baby sitter in Rhode Island — Emily always wanted to do these extra things for our mom and dad, being older I guess, so one day she decides we're going to scrub the kitchen floor. It sounds boring and all, but it ended up kind of fun, see, because she took some string and tied these wood-backed scrub brushes like skates to Charlie's and my feet, and then she poured the cleaning stuff all over the floor and turned on the radio, and we had a dance contest. Charlie and I were doing the twist and all these other dances and Emily was using the mop as the announcer's microphone . . ." I look over and notice Mary Jane's not really paying any attention to my story. Her eyes stare across the lock in a sort of vague distant way.

"It's hard to picture Charlie doing something so goofy. He used to be a lot more, though. Goofy, that is," I say quietly, more to myself.

"Goofy," repeats Mary Jane. I guess she's thinking about that jump.

From above, Ted's tucked body hurtles past us and cannonballs into the water.

"He was younger then," Rat says. His voice startles me; it takes me a second to realize he's talking about Charlie. I didn't think he was even listening to us.

"Yeah," I agree.

Charlie's whoop fills the air as he whistles down, following Ted's splash. Their laughter rises up to us from the water. Dan and Steph jump together, holding hands and howling to their double splash.

"Ted and Charlie even jumped off near the Culebra Cut last year," I mention. "Charlie said it was better than this jump because it's higher and it's more natural, off a cliff."

"Jumping off this tower, or even Culebra, doesn't seem so much fun to me," Rat remarks. He's so close that I can feel his breath, like dew on my cheek as he talks.

"No." I stretch out my arms and sit up. "I'd rather listen to the quiet." And yet, peaceful as it looks, the lock itself, dug out of the earth and soundlessly brimming or sinking with its mechanical tides, is nothing but trouble. The Canal's the reason my family is here, the reason that all the military bases are here, the reason everyone's so mad at Jimmy Carter right now; because he's giving the Canal back to Panama. Supposedly the new agreements with President Torrijos say that by the end of this century no Americans should be in Panama at all. The news stories about the Canal seem so far away from the flat dark path of water stretched out in front of me.

"Sometimes I feel like we're a million miles away from everywhere, living here." I say, almost under my breath. "In a whole other land, off on our own practically forgotten about."

"Doubtful." Rat frowns at me. "The army's not forgetting about the canal anytime soon. We're here to protect and defend." He lifts up his chin in a way that reminds me of Steph. "We should keep the canal, anyhow."

"My dad says Americans run it way better since we have all the money. Jimmy Carter's just a crooked old peanut farmer. My dad said Jimmy Carter promised not to give away the Canal so that Americans would vote for him, and then he turned right around and gave it back like a true politician."

"My mom thinks Jimmy Carter's right," I say. "She thinks Americans take too much of what doesn't belong to us, so we have to start giving stuff back."

"Americans run the Canal better," Rat says soundly. "Everyone knows that."

"Jimmy Carter and my mom say the new treaty's only fair. I think so, too, actually," I say. I try not to sound too intense about my opinion, like the way Mom gets when she talks about the Canal — all emotional and quivery-voiced.

"We built it — or at least, we decided it should get built." Rat looks mad. "Teddy Roosevelt did, anyway, and we've owned it for almost a hundred years. It was U.S. dollars spent to build it, too. The Canal makes us a ton of money. It's the only way a ship can get from the Atlantic to the Pacific Ocean without going all around South Amer –"

"I know that, everyone knows that." I wave off his words. Anyone who lives here knows exactly how important the Panama Canal is; how much trade is cleared through its locks every day, how convenient it is for ships coming from east to west and back again. "All I'm saying, Rat, is the people who own the country should own the Canal. I mean, Americans would be mad if, say, French people and the French army came into Ohio or somewhere and started trying to run things. Right?"

Mary Jane nods to agree with me, but since her family's from Georgia, they're all pro–Jimmy Carter.

"Well, but what if French people were smarter, ran it better?" Rat insists.

"They're still in Ohio," I say. "Where they don't belong."

"I don't even think France has an army," Rat says, and turns his head to squint very hard at the darkening horizon.

"My folks don't really talk too much about the Canal," Mary Jane admits matter-of-factly. "But they'd be spitting tacks if they knew I was fixing to jump into Miraflores."

"Be a snap if you did it before," Rat assures her.

"True." She pushes up her sunglasses to the top of her head, catching some of her bangs back with them like a headband.

"I'll go up to the top with you," I say on impulse, although just the thought of the top of the Miraflores water tower scares me knock-kneed. "I'll give you a pep talk or something."

"That'd be real sweet of you, Lane." Mary Jane reaches over and touches my shoulder. Then she stands up with a little hop and hauls herself fast up the ladder to the top of the tower, leaving just Rat and me on the grill.

The tower vibrates as all the jumpers, soaking wet and shaking off water like dogs, climb back on. They rattle the built-in ladder rungs as they rise past us, this time to the very top of the tower where poor old Mary Jane is waiting. The whole thing with Mary Jane is starting to remind me of those girls that used to get pushed into volcanoes so that the village would have rain or good crops.

"Check it out!" Charlie's voice hollers over me. "Ocean liner! This guy's huge!" Rat and I have to stand up; our view isn't as good. We watch as the gray prow of the cruise ship appears from around a jut of land. It kicks up a white foam in its path and sends large waves pulsing out through the water. The men on deck look tiny as toys but we wave at them anyway, hoping they'll see us.

"You coming up?" I ask Rat.

"Nah, you go on," he says. He won't look at me, since he knows I know he's too scared.

"I'm not going up there to jump, you know. I'm way too scared to jump," I say.

"Then I hope you don't fall in," Rat says, looking out to the water. His eyes follow the big ship as it moves slowly past us and down the channel. His face keeps his thoughts secret. Maybe he's upset; with me going up he'll be left all alone, a little chicken on the midway ledge. "It's going to rain any second now," he remarks. "You guys better hurry."

I've never climbed to the very top of the tower, and once I set my foot onto the rusty rungs leading up, up, up, I feel like I might puke. My fingers wrap tight over the railing and I squeeze away visions of the water.

Once I'm at the top, though, my eyes spy the initials' board, which I'd always heard about. It's a small prize for letting myself get so far away from the water, but I'm glad to get a look. Everyone who's ever climbed up and jumped down has scratched something into a piece of weathered wood that's nailed crooked to the scaffold.

"Aha, I thought I'd never see the day Elaine Beck

stood on the top of this tower." Ted grins as I inch my way closer to Mary Jane. Her hands are sealed tight as Tupperware lids over a metal cross bar.

"I'm just here for M.J." I assure him, and everyone else. "I'm not jumping or anything."

"Climbing's half the battle, Lane-a-tic." Ted coaxes me. "I have my Swiss Army knife with me — let me add your initials after I'm finished with Dan's."

"Hey, you know what? Forget about me."

We all turn. Dan's face looks marshmallow white beneath his tan and he gives us a lopsided smile. "I can't jump it, at least not today anyway. For one thing I have an ear infection and I'm also not feeling that good," he apologizes to Steph. "My stomach. I think it was too many raviolis. So maybe next time." We're all quiet, embarrassed for him and his bad excuses.

"This ledge's too small for so many wimps," Steph grunts. "Who ever heard of climbing up and not jumping down?"

"Look, I *never* said I was going," I repeat. "I'm just here for Mary Jane."

"Scratch my initials in again." Charlie nudges Ted. "Since you don't have to do Dan's ones."

"You don't get to put 'em in twice, Charleston." Ted waves the knife high in the air. "Just the new people's initials, like M.J.H."

"Yeah, only brand-new jumpers who never jumped

before," Steph says, looking right at Mary Jane. She and Charlie move close to watch over Ted's shoulders as he begins to carve out the M, so careful you'd think he was some crazy old woodcarver, old Gepetto or something.

The sky has turned pencil gray. I sneak a look down at the shadowed water; so flat, it could be ice. Everywhere is the same color of gray and shadows; it makes me think of one of those fuzzy black-and-white war movies. When I was little, I used to think that the olden times were actually lived in black and white and that's why you never saw color. Now, looking at all the gray, I feel like *I'm* in olden times; it's kind of scary.

I turn to Mary Jane and try to smile as I search for more stories.

"Bjorn Borg, he's that tennis player right, with the long blond hair?" I say softly.

"Right, I know. Real cute." Mary Jane shifts closer to me.

"Well my baby sitter Emily and I thought he was so great; I even had a poster of him in my old room in Rhode Island. Emily always said she was going to marry him."

"Isn't he already married?" Mary Jane asks.

"Is he? I don't think he was when Emily liked him. But anyhow, we used to design wedding dresses on this special art paper that would turn to paint if you brushed over them with water, and Emily thought up this amazing dress once — she told me she was going to open a wedding boutique after she married Bjorn Borg, and I could go work for her. But that was a while ago, when we were living in Rhode Island." My mind washes over the dim old pictures in my memory. "I'd still like to work at a boutique, though."

"Except no one would ever hire you, because you're always shooting your mouth off," Charlie says under his breath.

"Why don't you shut up, Charlie?"

"Actually, I was thinking why don't you shut up, Lane?"

"Why don't you both shut up?" growls Steph.

"I can talk about whatever I want." I speak to the flints of Charlie's eyes. He doesn't move out of my stare, but then he leaps to where I'm standing and his hand grabs at me, his fingers lacing tight around my wrist like whipcord. I try to wrench myself free and he pinches his fingers in tighter.

"Excuse me, will you let go of my wrist?" I use a more sarcastic version of Steph's teacher-voice, but Charlie just smiles his happy delirious smile.

"Will you let go of my wrist?" he mimics.

"I'm not kidding, Charlie." I start flipping my wrist up and down furiously.

"I'm not kidding, Charlie." He's strong, stronger than I am, and he won't let go, although the fingernails of my free hand are now digging and prying at the human handcuff he has made.

"Cut it out, guys," Ted says, but his voice trickles in from a distance. It's just Charlie and me now. I can see a faint blue in Charlie's lips and in the dents just beneath his eyes; his entire body is trembling slightly from the cold of the water and the disappeared sun. He won't let go and I want to punch him. My trapped hand curls into a fist.

"I hate your voice." Charlie spits out the words. "And your stupid boring stories and your stupid boring worries and your dumb poster of Bjorn Borg."

"Let go of my wrist!"

"Why do you talk and talk when you know I can't listen to you? When you know I'm telling you in my head just shut up shut up shut up — talking about your baby sitter and stupid wedding dresses. Just shut up, okay? Just don't talk about stupid boring stupid stupid —"

"I can talk whatever, whenever, howev –"

"Stupid stuff when you know what that does when I hear those —"

"I completely hate you." My voice is only a soft shadow to the shapes my lips form. And in that next second, when we both know what he's going to do, when in his eyes the knowledge of what he is going to do is mirrored by my mind's vision of what I know he's going to do, I think, *Yes I do hate you.*

He leaps first, so that my resistance won't be any match against the weight of his body. His fingers unlock once I'm launched into the air. My head's full of screaming, but no sound comes out, like in those nightmares when you've lost your power to speak or to run or call for help. I fall without noise, watching Charlie fall with me in a blur of limbs and crazy eyes. And in that roaring silence before the Canal swallows me, I suddenly feel water everywhere, and I realize that it's raining. The drops spatter clean against my skin for an instant, and then I meet the water with a smack and a plunge.

10

Charlie's bobbing head is the first thing I see after I thrash myself up from darkness. My ears and nose and mouth are full of water, and I shoot out into the air and an explosion of noise that is the rain and me screaming at last. My scream is a relief, almost happy, but it scares my brother. I narrow my eyes against the rain, now gunning down on us in stinging pebbles, and lunge for him.

Charlie darts down under the surface and away from me in a fierce wiggle, swimming farther out from the tower. I'm sort of laughing, from relief I guess, as I beat through the water after him. I yank my head and look every which way to find him, but he's gone. I thrash my legs, hoping I'll ram into an eye, a leg, anything. In a weird way, though, I also want to shout, "I did it! I jumped!" and I'm sort of proud of myself, although jumping wasn't my choice.

Charlie's slick pale head surfaces again; now he is even farther out. I push myself closer to him, pumping my arms and legs. If I could get even a quick cuff on his ear or the back of his head I'd feel better. He's closer to me, this time, when he comes up for air.

A massive crash and then another, both from behind, veer me off-course and Charlie slips below the surface of the water just as Ted and Steph push up from it. They catch up with me in only a few, sure strokes.

"You okay?" Steph shouts hoarsely. The rain nearly drums out her words.

"Charlie!" I scream. But the rain and the water everywhere hides him from me.

"Take it easy, Lane. Your body's in shock. Link your hands around my chest and I'll swim you in." It annoys me when Ted talks like he's some doctor. I'm not in shock.

"I'm okay." I breathe.

But Ted takes hold of my arms anyway and ducks in front of me, repositioning himself so that he's dragging me along as he swims an awkward sidestroke back to the tower. Steph paddles next to us. My eyes comb the water for Charlie, but he can slip and glide underwater forever, furtive as a minnow. He's probably swimming right underneath us, all open-eyed and laughing. Still, every second he doesn't surface gets me feeling more uneasy.

"That was a crummy stupid thing Charles did," Ted shouts over his shoulder through the thrumming rain. "Way out of line, way *way* out of line."

"Soon as he grabbed you, Ted and I climbed to the midway and long-dived out," Steph tells me. "I *knew* Charlie'd do something crazy like try to drown you. Where'd that kid go, anyway?"

"How should I know?" I clamp my chattering teeth shut, but then my chin starts wobbling. The water is cold from below and above; gray sky and water make a box around us. I can taste the fishy warmth of the Canal water mixed in with the cool raindrops. "Maybe the Lightning Gods'll get him." I gulp out loud to Ted, who laughs and says, "Yeah!" too cheerfully; probably just glad I'm not crying. My eyes move restlessly, though, waiting for Charlie to come up for air.

"I guess you can put my initials up, though," I mention to Ted.

"Definitely, E.F.B." Ted nods. Steph's ears perk up.

"Oh, no way. Being pushed doesn't count," she says.

"Definitely it counts," Ted answers.

"Does not," she insists.

"You want to walk home?"

Steph opens and closes her mouth like a goldfish. For a second I'm so happy that I'm embarrassed and I dunk my smile underwater.

"You see Charlie?" I ask in the next moment. It's been a long time not to catch even one quick glimpse of him. The old electric charge of worry zaps through me. My mind starts picking through horrible possibilities and lands on one. "He was just kidding about alligators in the locks, right? It's not like they can get in here, right?"

"Give me a break," mumbles Steph. "I don't know who's crazier, you or him."

"Ted, is it true?"

"Oh yeah, Charlie's gourmet gator grub by now."

When I see him hunched up in the prow of the boat, separate from the others who have regrouped there, I try to keep the relief out of my face.

Mary Jane stands up in the boat when we get within earshot. "We all climbed down," she hollers through the rain. "How are you guys?"

"I'm okay." I unhook my arms from Ted's shoulders and climb aboard. Rat and Dan are using the emergency coffee cans to dipper out the water gushing into the boat. Ted pulls the throttle, which chokes, but then sputters to life in a surprised gasp.

"Good jump?" Charlie smiles.

"I'm telling Mom, just so you know," I say, and

then I refuse to look at him and sit as far away from him as the boat allows.

"Steph said she bet he was gonna try to drown you or something," Mary Jane giggles nervously. The relief that she herself escaped the jump hums from every inch of her skin. She darts a look over at Charlie and slides nearer to me. "He's pure sicko," she says close in my ear. "Must be the worst thing in creation being his sister."

"He's just short-tempered is all," I say tiredly.

Water is pouring on us like there's a giant pitcher in the sky. A wind has kicked up, too, sending the rain down in heavy slanted sheets. The beating of rain on water sounds like a million snapping twigs.

"I can't even *see!*" Ted cries, exasperated, trying to shake the water off his face. "Everyone keep your eyes peeled for the dock. Ay-ay-ay, I've never been so wet."

"Hey, Lanie," Charlie calls out to me through the noise. I ignore him.

I keep ignoring him through the truck ride back to Fort Bryan, too. I'm still pretty mad. Charlie doesn't say much, except once to laugh at a bad joke Dan tells. He laughs and squints at me through the rain, but I look away. Charlie hates being ignored.

Midway home, the rain finally lightens to a drizzle and then abruptly stops. The truck's flatbed drains out and the air smells like a perfume of soft wind and leaves. The sun reappears, bleached white in the sky and the breeze riffles against my cold wet skin. Ted stops the truck once, at a roadside *bohío* where we each buy a paper cup of orangeade and a sugar cake. I'm so hungry that it tastes amazingly good.

Above us a line of khaki-shelled helicopters rattle past, like a herd of flying armadillos. We watch their clattering path through the sky until they disappear.

" 'Bye, Dad," shouts Dan. "My dad's probably up there. He's flying today."

"Good thing he wasn't around to see you be such a wink earlier," comments Steph. She puts her hand on her stomach and whines, "Probably too many ravioooh-leees." Dan says a swear word that's meant just for Steph, but she just shrugs it off and looks at him like she thinks he's pathetic.

Steph's kind of pouty and quiet for the rest of the trip, though, probably mad that everyone panicked for nothing over Charlie's and my jump, that my initials are going up, and that Mary Jane never even jumped.

"I want to go back to the fort," Charlie calls to Steph and Ted in the cab of the truck when we're letting Mary Jane out at her house. "Check it out again."

"On your own time, Charleston," Ted retorts. "You know the way."

As she scrabbles out of the truck, Mary Jane taps

my shoulder and whispers to me. "Was it real scary, falling from so high up?"

"Not so bad." I shrug. "It was actually sort of a relief."

Mary Jane giggles. "What do you mean? No one said *you* had to jump." But I can't explain to her what I mean exactly.

"It's not so bad as I thought," I say again. "Now that it's done."

Steph leans out the window. "Tomorrow morning, M.J.," she warns. "Official do-over, especially since your initials are up as a lie. I'll call you tonight with the details and no winking out."

"That's right, my initials are up," Mary Jane repeats. She surprises me by giving Steph a smirking grin. "See y'all tomorrow then, maybe, unless my momma's gotta take me shopping in the morning." She sweeps her ugly fishnet purse over her shoulder and walks away before Steph can answer.

Rat and Steph and Dan all jump out at the Wagners' house. Steph lingers over the driver's side window, making plans with Ted for tomorrow's fort building; how to round up more kids, when to drive to Miraflores for Mary Jane's do-over; while Rat and Dan rinse their muddy legs and sneakers at the outdoor water spigot. My own sandals are a skin of slime beneath my toes.

"See you tonight," I say to Ted when he finally drops Charlie and me off. He flips the day pass off the dashboard and into my hands.

"Tell Lord Beck thanks for the loan," he says. "And hang in there, trooper."

"Yep."

"See ya later, bud." Charlie waves. Ted frowns slightly at Charlie and just barely waves back to him as he drives away. I feel better then, watching Charlie looking all sad at the truck's rear bumper. He knows Ted's disappointed in him.

I switch past Charlie up the walkway, my sandals squishing through the front hall into the house.

Marita is standing at the stove in the kitchen.

"Soon is dinner," she says, nodding to me. "*Ropa vieja* and broccoli, *flan* for dessert." She lifts a lid and the browning smell of simmering, peppered meat fills the kitchen.

"Hey, Lanie," says Charlie, following me into the kitchen. "I'm running out to have a look at our fort again. Wanna come?"

I don't answer him. Marita peers up from her cooking.

"I'm going to take a shower," I tell Marita. "I fell in the Miraflores lock today and I smell worse than Charlie's feet."

"Wanna come?" Charlie asks me again. Marita knits her eyebrows as she studies Charlie, then me.

"I'll set the table if you want, Marita, after my shower," I say. She nods.

"You two fighting?" she asks, switching her finger back and forth between us.

"I'm not," Charlie assures her.

"Charlie tried to kill me today, but oh no, that's not fighting. Thanks, Charlie, for making me see the difference." I turn around and stomp away to the bathroom, leaving him to explain himself to Marita.

11

My second shower of the day is warm and sudsy, to clean the moldy stink of the water off my skin and clothes and hair. I change into another sundress; it's too short and frayed around the buttons, but it's worn soft from many spins through the washer and dryer. I guess Nancy Drew would have slipped into a cool linen dress and low-heeled pumps for dinner and a party. For a minute, I look in my closet, wondering. Since the only linen thing I have is a black skirt that's too wrinkly, I decide to forget looking cool and linenish.

I set the kitchen table for the two of us and then go to my room. My letter to Emily waits for me, unfinished. I sit at my desk and stare at the paper and think about telling her about Charlie and how he's gone bonkers, pushing me off the tower. I pick up my pen and chew the end.

Guess what! I jumped off this really high tower into the water and so my initials are going on this cool board they have up there. I know it's hard for you to believe, since I never even went off the middle dive at the Fort Lowthrop pool, but I promise it's truly true! In other news, I have to report that I'm worried about Charlie. He thinks he can do anything, and Mom and Dad never seem to be around when he's acting his worst, like today while we all were

"Lane." I don't even notice Charlie until he is breathing over my shoulder. I jump and swing around in my desk chair, slamming my hand over my letter, and glare at him.

"Why are you in my room without knocking?"

"The fort," he says, his voice flat. "It's wrecked. They wrecked it."

We sprint out of the house together, tearing across the front and back lawns that divide First Street from Second, then Second from Third. My bare feet squish over lumpy mud and grass until I'm looking over a half-collapsed side of the fort.

"Kids from the other side," Charlie gasps between ragged breaths.

"Maybe so, maybe not." I stoop to examine one of the fallen boards. "This all might have come down in the rain."

"Lane, it's wrecked. No rain did this." Charlie picks up a long splice of wood and hurls it like a javelin across the grass. "Why won't they play fair? They're breaking the rules, why won't they just play fair?"

"Charlie, for one thing it's not about any rules and for another thing, with enough people it's easy to hammer it all back into place, and for *another* thing I really do think it was the rain that knocked it down."

Charlie folds his hands into fists and stretches his mouth into a lipless line. "I'll get him. That kid Jason McCullough who was in the tree. It was him who destroyed our fort, I bet. He'll wish he was never born, I'll get him so bad."

"You don't even know if it was Jason McCullough in the tree. Look, see how the wind must have blown all this over?" I point to the tipped over boards. "No kids did this, see?"

The rain turned the floor of our fort into a black batter of mud. I can't resist stepping into it, letting it ooze over the tops of my feet. It feels so good that I give a little from my grudge against Charlie.

"Stick your feet in." I point to mine. He looks at me and grins, then hops with both feet in the mud, spraying dark speckles all over my dress.

"Now look what you did!" I jump out of the puddle to the grass and try to brush off mud polka-dots, which just end up smearing.

"I'm sorry Lane, I didn't mean it." Charlie tries to help me, but his hands are damp and dirty from lifting the wet boards of the fort.

"Stop — you're making it worse." I push off his help and then leave him standing alone as I run back to the house. When I'm far enough away from him, my anger slows me down until I'm walking and muttering under my breath like a bag lady. Charlie can get on my nerves more than anyone else I know. I can't believe he made me come over here in the first place just to look at a little bit of stupid rain damage.

Dinner has been ready. I slip into my seat and pick up a fork. Marita leans against the counter, holding her paperback square in front of her eyes.

"Sorry I'm late," I mumble and quickly shovel a forkful of *ropa vieja* in my mouth.

"Where is Charlie?"

"Coming. He's outside." I chew and swallow in silence, staring at my plate. I feel Marita's eyes on me for a long minute, then she burrows back into her book.

"Sorry I'm late." Charlie speeds in from the kitchen door to his seat and smiles at me, but a worry wrinkle shows in his forehead. "How's your dress?"

"The same." I look down the front of my blotched dress.

"Sorry about that again, Lane. You know I didn't mean to mess it up."

"Mmmm-hmmm." I half-bow my head toward him, the way the Chinese people do after they sell you fruit or vegetables in the downtown market — distant-polite. Charlie apologizing twice for a dumb little thing like getting mud on my dress, but refusing to even acknowledge a big thing like practically trying to kill me is another snarled string of Charlie-logic; it makes me mad, knowing this is the best he can do.

"I'm going to go beat up that kid after dinner," he mutters behind his hand to me so that Marita can't hear.

"Which kid? Jason McCullough?"

"Of course him. And if it wasn't him throwing those mangoes" — Charlie pauses dramatically to pop a broccoli tree in his mouth — "then I'll beat on him until he snitches." He clenches his hand and raises it into the air. "Heigh-ho, Sil-ver!" he shouts. "The Lone Ranger" comes on TV at five o'clock every Sunday, and Charlie and I never miss it since it's one of the only our-age programs aired.

"That's one of the advantages of living in this country," Dad told us once. "Classic all-American programming." He said this like outdated old "Lone

· 120 ·

Ranger" and "Flipper" and that annoying Zsa-Zsa in "Green Acres" are all some special treat. Charlie and I both think the Lone Ranger's a dork and we always say "Heigh-ho, Silver!" as a joke to each other. But the military broadcast services believe in getting classic all-American programming out to everyone.

"Oh what, you're just going to walk up to his house and knock on his door and say, 'Oh, hi, I'm Charlie Beck and if you're Jason McCullough I'm here to beat you up?' That sounds like a really smart idea, Charlie."

"No, *cucaracha*, tonight I'm going to go to their fort to hide." He quirks his eyebrows up and down like Groucho Marx. "I'll hang out in the tree and wait and then — a commando surprise attack on the wing." He shapes his thumb and pointer finger into a gun and makes a clicking noise with his tongue. "Gotta love it," he says.

"You're imitating Ted."

"So?" he lifts his chin. "Anyhow, tonight don't tell Ted about my plan 'cause he'll want to come with me."

"He will not — he'll tell you not to be *loco*, climbing up trees late at night when you'll get bug-bit to death plus you can't see anything. Charlie, you're making too much out of it."

I suddenly notice Marita's listening. I drop my voice and lean in very close to Charlie's ear. "I mean, building the fort's really just for us, dummy. It's not like we're really going to kill those kids from the other side or they're really planning to get us. It's just good to have a fort to go to and make better and stronger and stuff. You — you're the only one who thinks it's some kind of war. Even Steph knows better."

"What fighting kids?" Marita's alert, looking at Charlie, who stares down at his plate and says nothing. "Lane, you fighting with who, what kids?"

"I'm telling Charlie not to fight with some stupid kids he wants to beat up," I explain. I feel sort of like a tattletale, but maybe just the threat of Marita's knowing something will stop him. Charlie crosses his arms over his chest and tips himself back onto the hind legs of his chair. He watches me with eyes like pinpricks.

"Don't worry about it, Marita," he scowls. "No one's fighting anyone. It was just something I was thinking about for a minute." But I can hear the lie hanging in the words that don't even sound like Charlie's own.

"So that means you're not going to hike all the way to Ninth Street and hide out in a tree, even though the rule is no going out after dinner?" I ask brightly, for Marita's benefit.

Charlie's scowl deepens.

"Ninth Street?" Marita grates back her chair and stands to clear the table. "No no no, Charlie, or I am telling Señora. Too far and dark for fighting." She exhales heavily. "You both of you are" — she twirls a finger in the air — "spinning very fast, always, close to trouble. *Opino que ustedes, los dos, necesitan ayuda.*"

"What did you say? I need your opinion?" asks Charlie.

"She said, 'I think Charlie needs help,' " I answer.

"She did not. She did not say Charlie." He crunches up his napkin and beams it at me. It hits my nose and drops into my plate. "She said, 'Lane has fish eyes and scabby knees.' "

"She said Charlie deserves to be slow-roasted on a spit and served to Cat Face, Rat Face, and The Toothless Wonder for lunch," I reply.

Charlie almost spits out his milk through his nose, laughing. Cat Face is what we named our slobby school bus driver who fights with Charlie almost every day because he never sits down in the same seat for the entire ride. Rat Face and The Toothless Wonder are our names for her two little kids, who sit in the front seat. Cat Face feeds them candy all day, so they stay quiet.

"She said, 'Lane is a skunk-faced, bug-eyed, sloth-bodied —' "

"*Bastante*, both of you. Ay-ay-ay." Marita lifts our empty plates from the table and clatters them in the sink. "I am going to do laundry. Dessert is there for both." She taps the dish of custard sitting on the counter. "No fighting, or I tell Señora. Sometimes I think even all the laughing is *loco*, too much . . ." She shakes her head at us, but keeps her unfinished thought hovering in the air as she leaves the kitchen.

12

Charlie and I use up about five minutes splitting the custard, so that we each get exactly equal shares. Then we have a speed-eating contest that gives me a stomachache. After dinner, feeling full as two stuffed potatoes, we sit in the den and play a round of Clue, but it's too easy to guess the murderer with only two of us playing.

"We need a third," Charlie mumbles. I think of my letter to Emily resting unfinished on my desk.

"Mom said she and Dad were coming home from the change of command at seven-thirty."

"When's the last time Mom and Dad ever played Clue?" Charlie tosses down his cards. "Mr. Green," he says sourly. "In the ballroom with the rope. Bore-ring." He slides to his hands and the balls of his feet and starts pumping himself through a round of pushups.

"I have the ballroom." I wag the card in his face. "So I win, I win. You guessed wrong."

"Big deal. It's not like you get a prize."

"You shouldn't exercise so soon after dinner."

"I have to get in shape for later," Charlie huffs. "But thanks for one more tip about what I'm not allowed to do, Miss Rules."

"I swear I'll tell Ted exactly where you are if you leave tonight. He'll tell Mom."

"So tell," Charlie puffs.

"He'll make you come back."

"He's the one who wants to go back with me tomorrow and get those kids. It's not true what you said, that building the fort's just for us. It's our protection against the other side. You never know when they're planning to strike, like the commies."

"That's so mature, Charlie. I feel so much safer, knowing you're defending me from commies."

"Look, bug-eyes, why don't you shut up and butt out?" He sits on his knees, panting.

"Shut up, Charlie. Why don't you learn how to act older than a three-year-old?" I climb to my feet and head for the door.

"Well, I'm not cleaning up this stupid game, since it was your idea to play," he says. He kicks away the game board with his heels, sending it skidding into the side of my foot.

"Ouch!" I yell. "What's your problem?" As I walk past him to the door, my upper leg brushes hard against his shoulder, enough to knock him off balance.

"Cut it — out!" He reaches up with both hands to shove me into the doorframe and I stub my toe.

I'm just about to shove him back when I hear the sound of the front door. I leap out the den to safety and run to greet Mom.

"Chicken chicken chicken!" I hear him yell from the den.

"Lane, were you worrying?" Mom looks stern and checks her wristwatch. "Because I told you by eight and it's not eight yet."

"I wasn't worrying. I never worry until it's later than what you say."

"I don't know if that's exactly the answer I was looking for." She nips up my chin with her index finger. "Goofy girl. You're going to give yourself an ulcer. I really am thinking about Dr. Forrest again."

"Where's Dad?"

"Dad stayed at the Officer's Club and I can't give you an exact time when he'll be home, so don't ask, but you can do some more useless worrying about him if you'd like. Or you can help me by getting out the silverware and linen for the party. Where's Charlie?"

"Den."

Mom nods and clanks her car keys into the china bowl on the hall table, where she always keeps them. She places her purse carefully beside the bowl and drifts into the living room.

"Here we are in November and it's still light out," she remarks, staring out the window at nothing in particular. "We never get that horrible winter-dark here. Isn't that nice?"

"I guess."

"So pretty and colorful. Always sunshine." She half-closes her eyes and smiles, and I recognize in her smile the same expression Charlie makes before he does something wild.

"No snow, no ice." I say, thinking about the accident. My words must make Mom think about it, too. She steps back from me like I just sneezed with my mouth open; like I did something wrong to her.

"Lane, do me a favor?" she says.

I nod. Mom smiles and the moment's okay again. "If you do the table, I'm just going to have a shower and change."

"Sure."

"That'd be great." Mom smoothes my hair back behind my ears and then wanders away from me, thinking of other things. She sheds her sandals and carries them with her as she walks along the edge of the living room carpet and up the stairs.

Our corner cupboard holds all the glasses and plates and tablecloths, as well as a scratched wooden chest filled with splotched silver forks and knives and odd-sized spoons. I open the chest and scoop up fistfuls of silverware, plunking them down in a line on one end of the dining room table. No matter how much Marita polishes it, the silver is always tarnished olivey-gold. I don't like eating with real silver, anyway. It makes my food taste cold.

I pick up one of the larger spoons, rub it with the hem of my dress and peer into the upside-down pinched face shining back at me. My face looks pointed and mean, like a witch, but I definitely don't have bug-eyes. "Jerk," I mutter, setting the spoon down.

Wine glasses are next. I stand them in rows like soldiers. The hand-embroidered napkins and placemats are last to come out. We have too many, since we can buy them for cheap downtown, and all my aunts and uncles in the States got them for Christmas last year because they're really expensive up there. They are so beautiful, though — birds and flowers and fruits stitched in silk on linen, each one unique as a snowflake. I begin to fold them one by one into flat fan shapes the way Marita does.

"What day is it?" Charlie has been watching me from the door. I jump.

"Why do you always scare me like that? Friday."

"Everything scares you, Lame. Don't they always go out on Friday and have parties on Saturday?" He walks slowly around the room, bumping his hand along the carved backs of the dining room chairs.

"Except they went out last night so the party's tonight."

"Where'd they go last night?" Charlie stops in front of his reflection in the mirror over the sideboard and knobs up the muscles of his arms. "Like I need jungle fruit to look like this, ha."

"I don't know. Other parties? How would I know?"

"Is this going to be a loud one like last week, where we can't sleep even with our doors shut?"

"I hope not, and I hope not too many people come."

"Too many people always come."

"You know, we never used to have these parties until we came here."

"Gee, Lane. We never used to do lots of things until we came here. You're such a genius to notice. Hey, you know what I hate?" He has stopped in front of Mom's painting, a picture of a bowl of peaches that she did last year when she was taking this art class at the Rec Center.

"What?"

"That painting. I hate how Mom never finished that last peach." I walk over to where he's standing and look, too, although I know what he's talking about. All the peaches are nestled in a blue bowl by a window. The unfinished peach is in the back, like a smooth bald baby head among all the brushed oil colors. "I hate that this painting's, y'know, hanging up on our wall, when it's not finished yet, just because Dad decided it was finished."

"Well, it was Mom who didn't finish it," I say.

"But it was Dad who hung it up," Charlie answers. His nose is practically touching the painting. "It's like a ghost peach," he decides, turning away from it, his hands on his hips, like he just figured out a math equation on the blackboard.

"Alexa just pulled in," I say.

Through the dining room window, I watch her two-seater sports car screech to a stop in the carport. Linda sits in the passenger seat. A red-and-white-striped catering truck from Diferente follows behind.

"I'm going to finish my F15 model." Charlie jumps for the door. "It's almost done. Come in and look when you're done with all that." He hightails it before he has to say hello to Alexa.

13

"Yoo hoo!" Alexa calls from the hallway. Her perfume enters the room before she does. It smells sweet, like Hawaiian Punch. "The food followed me here," she calls out to no one in particular. "And I brought Linda to help out. Where's Marita? *¿Estás aquí*, Marita?" Alexa sees me and flows into the dining room, trailed by Linda, who's wearing a crisp beige uniform and is holding another crisp beige uniform in a see-through dry cleaning bag.

Marita won't be happy; the uniform is for her to wear tonight. Mom and Dad never ask Marita to wear a uniform. When we first came here, they both were strict about telling Charlie and me to be polite to everyone's housekeepers; to say "please" and "thank you" to Marita and not to use words like "maid" or "our girl." But Alexa handles housekeepers differently and tries to overrule Mom's opinions, always supervising Marita, making her do extra stuff and wear the beige uniform.

"I guess she's in her room. And Mom's showering and getting ready."

"We're in a crisis," bubbles Alexa, "because I can't find any Bug-Be-Gone candles. I hit all the PX's on all the bases and of course there's nothing, which again proves my theory that the PX is run by true military intelligence — ha!" She gives a meaty laugh and then begins pointing and jabbering at Linda in her flat dubbed Spanish that's too fast for me to understand. Linda nods, then slips away.

I close the corner cupboard and brush my hands together. "I've set up the table for the buffet. Dad's still at the change of command party. Do you want something to drink?"

"No, sweetie, I'll have Linda make me a drink — she knows how I like them — strong!" Alexa touches both her hands to her left ear and secures the backing of one of her snail-sized gold earrings. "Now tell me. Where's your mother?"

I sigh, wondering how Alexa can stand in front of me and give me all the evidence that she's listening, but then never have any memory of what I've said to show for it.

"I'm here, Al. Did you remember candles? The table looks nice, Lane." Mom breezes into the room, smiling in her best hostess style. Her hair's wet and she's dressed in a pair of Dad's old loafers paired with his oversized faded chinos and an oxford shirt unbuttoned to the grainy freckles of her chest. Her belt is pulled into the last hole and the pants' fabric bunches in lumpish pleats. All Dad's castoffs. In a way, she can make me see the way Dad might have looked when he was young, before he bulged out.

"No candles anywhere on any base! We have to go on another mission downtown!" Alexa loves a crisis.

"The catering truck is here," I say. "Marita probably needs help organizing."

Mom looks from Alexa to me and then decides. "Okay, we'll go downtown, and Lane, you supervise the food. Just make them put it all in the kitchen for now and then Marita — is Linda here?" Alexa nods. Mom continues, "And Marita and Linda will change the foil plates to china plates and make the food look pretty, which is all that really needs to be done." She turns to Alexa. "You know, if we can't find candles we won't be able to use the back porch."

"What about your tiki lamps?" asks Alexa.

"We had some, yes, but I don't know where I put them." Mom crinkles her eyebrows together and up, like she's mystified, although she and I both know that last month in a fit of boredom or evil Charlie dropped each tiki lamp off our roof one by one, watching them smash on the pavement below. Dad and Mom grounded him for three days. Mom tries to suppress tales of Charlie's tantrums whenever she can.

After Alexa and Mom speed off in Alexa's car in search of candles, I go out to the kitchen. Linda and Marita are unpacking the boxes of food the caterers have hauled in from the Diferente truck through the back door of the kitchen. Marita has changed into the beige uniform and her long black hair is rolled into a hairnet, in the same style as Linda.

"Can I help?" I ask. "Mom said if you needed help to ask me."

"We're fine." Linda makes the okay sign with her hand and Marita laughs and makes the sign, too. "Okie-doke!" she says through her nose, I guess imitating an American voice. They both look at each other and laugh. I feel stupid without really knowing why.

The counter is chock-full of food — plates of teriyaki chicken and steamed vegetables and rice and marinated steak, plus platters of bite-sized food held together by frilly-capped toothpicks.

Marita slides the food onto china dishes while Linda cuts the stems off a pile of fresh flowers and arranges the blossoms around the plates. They chatter together, their words only understood by me in crumbs and edges.

"Well, I'm going to go, then," I say. I feel way out of place. I make the okay sign, which starts them laughing again.

"Almost time for bed," Marita calls out to me as I'm leaving. "Put that dress in the washroom for me to clean the mud off it later."

"Yep. *Buenas noches.*"

"Good night," they chorus.

Charlie's room smells like airplane glue and his finished F15 model sits proudly on the landing strip of his desk, but he's nowhere in sight. Next to the plane is a folded piece of paper. I open it and read:

Lane,

I have already gone on a commando mission to the other side to get that dumb kid Jason Mikulluh. I'm going to counter attack which will be a big surprise which he's not expecting. I'm writing so you don't get all worryed like a crybaby about where I am, but if you tell Mom or Dad or Marita, I will be REALLY pist off. If I need back up, I will come back for you and Ted by 21:00.

Over and out

C. G. Beck

14

I crinkle the letter into one hand and run out of his room, out the front door, and onto the front lawn. The sky is smudged deep blue with the beginning of night and the heavy air is warm as breath.

"Charlie, can you hear me? If you're out there, tell me. Mom's going to be mad — the rule is no going out after supper. Can you hear me?" The darkness erases my words into a bleat. I hear crickets and smell bug spray, but I don't see Charlie anywhere. "Don't you do anything stupid, Charlie," I call. "You just better not do that to me."

I turn back to the house and spy Marita in the window, bent over the sink. The catering truck's gone. Twin beams of car headlights flash in the distance and I watch as Dad's jeep pulls into view, flooding the street with a pool of electric yellow.

"Is that you, Lanie?" he asks when he shuts the

engine. "What are you doing; decided to bring your worries out for an airing?"

"Not really."

"Then what really?" Dad's voice is loudly cheerful. His arms are weighted down with two brown paper bags and he slams the door of the jeep with his boot.

"Nothing I guess. I was just going in." I follow him into the house, into the den where he deposits the bags on the bar. He pulls out all the bottles from the bags and sets each bottle neatly on the glass bar shelf with the others. Rows and rows and rows of bottles, all sizes and shapes.

"That ought to get this crew through tonight, anyway," he says, surveying the shelf, satisfied.

"How was the change of command party?" I ask.

"So-so. Got more fun later. The thing was . . ." He strides out of the den, so that I have to tag along behind.

"Was what?" I trail him upstairs and into his and and Mom's bedroom, where he starts to depin his buttons and tags and medals from his dress blue uniform, carefully dropping each item into Mom's open jewelry box.

"That we were all sad to see Major Gregory leave for Fort Ord, and we're not so excited about Jacobs taking over Alpha Company, so while the ceremony and party were nice, it marks the beginning of a not-so-fun time for Alpha. And some of the younger guys were . . ." He shakes off his dress jacket and disappears into the walk-in closet.

"Were what?" No response. I pick up one of Dad's pins — it's actually just a name tag — Lt. Col. Beck. Everywhere I go here, I am glued to that name. It's stuck to my house, my ID, my passport, all my forms for school. Lt. Col. Beck's dependent; that's how the army catalogs Charlie and Mom and me. I drop the tag back in Mom's jewelry box.

"Were what?" I ask louder. Dad pokes his head out of the closet.

"What were what?" he asks. "Where's Mom?"

"She and Alexa went to buy candles. Downtown."

"Lane, you're going to have to scram now while I get ready, okay?"

"I'm going to bed." *After Charlie comes back. Please come back Charlie.*

"Good idea." His head disappears again.

The downstairs seems extra spacious, and I realize the coffee table and the end tables are missing from the living room. Party-proofing, Alex calls it, when you hide your furniture from rowdy guests who might scuff or break or burn their cigarettes on it. I didn't notice it missing before; and now I wonder where the furniture got stored. I tour through the rooms, opening doors, aimlessly looking for it.

I find everything piled and stacked perfectly into the impossibly small space of our coat closet. Mom must have done it herself; her mind knows exactly how to wrap around problems of squares and spaces and angles. I imagine all those math-teacher rules boxed-up and gathering dust in a corner of her mind. She liked teaching, but after the accident she decided that facing a classroom of ninth graders each day was too much to handle. "Too much to think about," she told me. Her teacher's clothes and books are neatly packed away with all our winter stuff in storage chests at my grandparents' house.

It would be nice to see my winter things again. I miss my navy blue wool coat with red piping, although I bet it's too small for me now and moths have likely eaten holes in it. I miss my ice skates, too, although I was always too chicken to do more than shuffle around the edge of the pond in them; and I'd like to see my Swiss hat with the attached braids again.

I used to wear that hat even in the summer, pretending with my dolls that I was Heidi sitting on the Alps, drinking my milk out of a soup bowl, and eating big hunks of cheese until Emily and her friends' teasing — they'd yodel, "yoo-hoo-loo-oo — ser" — made me have to hide my milk and cheese parties in my room.

"If I don't see a winter for the next twenty years, it will be too soon," Mom had said when the last box was packed, her words sealing shut my hopes of ever going back to Rhode Island. I'd never gotten attached to any one place. Before Rhode Island we'd lived in Tennessee, before that Georgia, before that Washington, before that Virginia, where Charlie was born and back as far as I can remember, though I was born in South Carolina. But, still, I hope I see winter sometime in the next twenty years.

I go back up to my room and fasten the lock on my door. My letter to Emily is dumb when I reread it. I can't remember how I'd been planning to finish off the now-broken sentence I had started before Charlie interrupted me. I cross out the last sentence and write instead:

> *Now Charlie is missing because he went to beat up some dumb old kid. I have to think about how to get him home, so I'm signing off now.*
>
> *With so much love from,*
>
> *Lanie*

When I tear out the letter I notice there's almost no paper left, just a lot of scraggledy edges from where

I've torn out pages. It scares me all of a sudden, seeing all those crooked jags where paper used to be. The book was so thick; I never thought I'd use all the paper. I close the journal and stare for a long time at the girl in the tulip who Emily said looked like me.

I fold the letter into an envelope, then take a long time writing Emily's name on the front in calligraphy letters. Emily had taught me calligraphy when she got a set for Christmas, but I used to write it so blobby and messy. Once I wrecked one of her best calligraphy pens and she cried and didn't talk to me all day. I can still see that pen, its smushed-up tip dripping over with blue ink from where I pressed too hard. She had called me a klutz, but that was a long time ago and now I have my own pens and I'm very good. Very very careful. I replace the journal under my mattress and set the envelope on the corner of my desk to let the ink dry.

"Where are you, Charlie?" I ask out loud. Cars have been pulling up to the house, doors thud shut, and voices of men and women are laughing and calling out each other's names as their footsteps clack up to our house. Dad has turned on the hi-fi, and soon the house is steaming over with the energy of people who want to dance and talk and eat too much.

I lie on my bed and pick up my Nancy Drew book. The jewel smugglers just found out that Nancy is not a belly dancer, but a girl detective, and so now they're in hot pursuit. I work to focus on the printed words, but the downstairs is becoming way too noisy. Mom and Alexa have returned, I hear Alexa shout — "We found them, and we bought hundreds!" and then the voices slowly begin sliding over to the outside of the house as people gather on the porch. Dishes and glasses clatter and clink and everyone's all mouth to me, laughing and talking and eating.

I try to identify voices. I hear Dee and then Ted, but I don't want to leave my room and say hi. Ted and his other group of Zonie friends can move into the land of adults in a way that makes me feel like a dorky military kid.

I hear a tapping on my door.

"Come in." The door opens a little and Mom's face peeks through the slivered space. Her cheeks are pink.

"Lane, if it gets too loud, and you and Charlie want to, then Mrs. Davidson says you both can sleep at their house next door in their spare room."

"Okay, maybe I will."

"Where's Charlie?"

"Bathroom." I look down at my book. "Good night Mom."

"We found candles at this awful little store off the Tumba Muerto," she says.

"It sounds like a big party, huh? Too many army wives?"

"Oh, they're no big deal . . ." Mom's smile reveals her teeth but not her thoughts.

"Well, good night then, Mom." I look down. The page blurs in front of my eyes and I blink to refocus. Mom lingers and I feel her staring at me, unfixed about what else to say but not wanting to leave me just yet.

"So remember to tell Charlie when he comes out of the bathroom. About the Davidsons."

"I will."

"But check in with me if you do go, so I know."

"Yep."

"Good night, Lane. Love you."

"Love you, too." I look up to smile at her pink-cheeked smile but she's already shut the door.

15

After Nancy escapes the jewel thieves and is reunited with her father, the distinguished attorney Carson Drew, I get up and walk into the bathroom to brush my teeth. A moth bats against the fluorescent lighting; its blue-white tract hums along with the moth's bump and whirring. I shove open the bathroom window and switch off the light.

"Stupid moth," I say. "Shoo." Maybe the moonlight is bright enough to draw the moth back outside. But when I switch back on the light, the stupid moth hasn't moved, and starts its dance again. "Your funeral," I tell it, trying to sound casual, but in my heart I'm worried. I brush my teeth quickly so that I can turn the light off again, and when I come back to my room Ted, changed into a nonwrinkled shirt and shorts, is sitting on my bed reading my book.

"You are a Nerd with a capital N," he says,

grinning. "How many of these Nancy Drews do you read a week?" He tosses me the book, which I catch and hold against my chest.

"As many as the library lets me have. Are Hans and Court here?" Hans and Courtland are Ted's two older friends from the Zone. They're Ted's best Zone friends — sophomores in high school — and they'd only ever talk to me if Ted were around. I'm actually pretty scared of them, and if they're roaming through my house I need to be forewarned.

"Yep, the two stooges — out on the porch being buffoons, lying to your mother and my mother about how good they're doing in school. Where's Port Charlie?"

I can't answer with a lie and I can't answer with the truth so I don't say anything.

"Are you deaf?"

"He went for a walk."

"At nine o'clock at night? Where did he have to go walk to?"

I don't answer, but I'm relieved. Ted's guessed immediately.

"Oh, don't even tell me. He went to the other side to do some damage to the fort, right?" Ted stands up and exhales so hard that I see his nostrils flare out. "When did he leave?"

"Forty minutes ago."

Ted checks his watch. "Okay, so we'll wait half an hour and then go get him. I'm going to give myself the benefit of thinking all that's really going to happen is that Charlie'll run all the way over to the other side, kick the side door of the fort a few times, throw a few mangoes at the tree, and run home with his arms in the air like Rocky. Safe bet?"

"I guess so. See, some boards of our fort fell down — from the rain I guessed — and Charlie's all mad, thinks it was Jason McCullough behind it."

"Yeah, I stopped and looked at our fort with Court and Hans on the way over. It's easy to fix, plus those guys want to work on it, too. We're going to double-enforce it with two different kinds of wood."

"Um, good." I wind my hair up off my neck and nervously start twisting it into a crooked braid. If Hans and Court are planning to work on the fort, then there won't be any room for girls — except maybe girls like Steph. It's a depressing thought. "I guess we can wait half an hour."

"Have you eaten? Great food tonight. Better than last night's spread at the Horowitzes'." Ted slips his fingers back through his hair. "Do I look okay? Jennifer Elwig's here."

"She's a junior in high school, big shot. Two grades over you." I reach up and pluck a piece of fuzz off his shirt collar. "You look okay for a dork."

"Come out and chow down with me when you're tired of reading," Ted messes up my hair with both hands. "And don't freak out about Charlie. He always comes home eventually, right?"

"Right."

And then Ted is gone. Now I feel like a prisoner in my room, knowing that Hans and Courtland are tracking through my house in their big basketball sneakers, their mouths full of food and critical comments.

Hans and Courtland and most Zonian kids over age fourteen show up at any party they can get to on-base, because basically all Zonians do almost everything together. Dad says it's ridiculous that the Zonian adults and kids go to the same parties. The typical schizophrenia, he says, of people who have no true culture.

After forty-two minutes of trying to read and then sketching lopsided old wedding dresses — I am definitely rusty at my drawing — I can't stand it anymore. I'll have to face the party to retrieve Ted so we can find Charlie.

"Of course it's not like anything really bad will happen to him," I mutter to steady my nerves. "Nothing bad will ever *really* happen if I think through all the possibilities of what *might* happen."

"Well, Lane, what are you doing still up?" asks Mrs. Wagner when I slink down the hall. She sits in the middle of a packet of army wives in a circle of chairs that have been rearranged in the living room. Their dinner plates are balanced neatly on their knees, their heads and shoulders are all hunched forward and drawn in together like spokes of a tepee.

"Hi, Mrs. Wagner. I'm just about to go to bed now. Hi, everyone." The army wives murmur and smile and dip their heads. Aside from their whispering campfire, no one else is in the room.

"Well, your mama's on the porch, honey, if you need her. And I think your dad's in the den with the other men," says a lady whose name I've forgotten from when I met her at the last party. Her thick glasses shrink her eyes to the size of little gerbil droppings.

"I'm actually looking for Ted Tie," I answer. The lady frowns.

"Is he part of that group of kids from the Zone who are here? I just saw them all come in for more food at the buffet." She cranes her neck to look into the empty dining room. "They're not in there anymore."

"I declare it's a mighty strange thing, having these Zone kids running loose in an adult's party," mentions another wife with a clown-orange tan.

"Zonians keep clear of military, generally speaking," Mrs. Wagner says in a voice that seems to mean that Zonians are awed and scared of military. Mrs.

Wagner likes thinking that everyone's awed and scared of military.

"Your friend is most likely out on the porch with all the other Zone people," says gerbil eyes. "If you see your mother, tell her that Arlene White — Colonel White's wife — would love to get hold of the recipe for that yummy steak marinate."

"I will. See you later, then. Good night, everybody." I speed away from the wives with a sigh of relief. If they ever knew that Mom had the party catered, they'd go on about it for weeks. Better just let Mom win a few good points with the wives and let them all think she's some great chef.

16

I see Courtland and Hans sprawled in on the wide doorframe of the sliding glass door that leads from the living room out to the porch. They're rifling through an orange crate of Dad's record albums and arguing about what to put on the hi-fi next. I skirt past them. I don't want to ask them about Ted. Ted himself is nowhere in sight. My nerves rattle like a box of tacks. If Ted forgot and already left the party, then how will I find Charlie?

The candles keep away the mosquitoes but not the dark, so it's hard to pick out faces as I scout through the crowd. It seems like hundreds of Zonians have willingly crunched themselves onto the porch so that they can be with just each other and away from the army wives. I strain my neck above the crowd and almost bump into Jennifer Elwig.

She raises her plucked-to-dental-floss-thin eyebrows

high and stares down at me like she's never seen me in her life. My face gets red, knowing I have to talk to her now, and I'm glad for the darkness.

"Have you seen Ted Tie?"

"What?"

I cough. "Ted Tie. Have you seen him anywhere?"

"It's not like I'm exactly looking for him." She yawns. Ted probably wouldn't be happy to hear her say that. Jennifer shakes her long feathered hair back behind her head. "You're Abby's oldest kid, right?" she asks.

"Yeah." I'm wondering if I should tell Ted what she just said, or if I should keep quiet.

"Abby's a scream. She's over there, if you're interested." Jennifer points to the far side of the porch and I can just glimpse Mom's spiky hair behind a clump of other ladies.

"I'm looking for Ted actually, just Ted."

"Why do you need him? Hey, you got a crush on him or something?" An annoyingly sly smile begins to expand over Jennifer's face. "He's a cutie."

"I don't even — I mean I would never ever even . . ." Jennifer's smile flusters me. I want to think up something clever, something Nancy Drewish, to say back to her. "Oh, Ted's just a chum." I try to laugh cunningly like Nancy. "I wouldn't even imagine —"

"Okay, whatever." Jennifer's already scanning the

crowd for better company. I mumble goodbye and duck away from her, skating through the crowd. "Chum!" — how did I let myself say that? It seems normal when Nancy Drew says it, but in real life it's completely dumb. I could kick myself. Dumb old Jennifer Elwig.

"Whoa, Lane, what are you still doing up?" Mom catches my arm as I slide by. No Ted, no Ted anywhere. Where could he have gone? "Are we getting too loud for you, sweetie? Are you going to the Davidson's? Aren't you tired? It's getting late."

"I was just . . . um." I began to bite at the skin next to my fingernails. I'm tired. The weight of the day feels like it's collapsing on me. It would be nice to go sleep at the Davidson's, where it's quiet.

"I was just telling Alexa and Dee and Greta about the time Mina and Pops had the butterfly party." Mom's talk is happy and loose; she pulls me next to her and I am caught in her story. The ring of Alexa and Dee and Greta's faces shine with drop-mouthed smiles, ready to laugh. Mom knows how to tell lots of funny stories, but I've heard this one before. It goes like this: A long time ago, way before I was born, Mina and Pops had a big garden party and shipped in hundreds of butterflies from some foreign country, but on the day of the party, when they released them from the boxes, the butterflies flopped out into the air for about two seconds and then dropped dead on all the guests' heads.

When Mom first told Emily and Charlie and me that story, I remember it was summertime and we were sitting around the kitchen table, even Dad, eating wild raspberries. Charlie and Mom had laughed so hard, red berry-mouthed laughs — but Emily started pounding her fists on the kitchen table, hollering, "Why didn't anyone punch holes? Why didn't anyone remember to punch holes in the boxes?"

She got up from the table and slammed herself into the bathroom. Mom followed her and stood outside the bathroom saying, "Come on, please, Emmy, come out of there. It's just a silly story. I'm sorry, Em. I should remember about you and animals," while she and Dad made funny faces at each other like, isn't she crazy? I just sat in my chair, splitting a raspberry seed between my teeth, feeling bad and keeping quiet.

Now I wonder if Mom remembers about Emily and the bathroom when she tells the butterfly story.

Alexa and Dee and Greta all end up laughing, but Greta keeps repeating oh, that's terrible, that's too terrible. Mom laughs, too, from the sheer comfort of talking about Virginia. Her million everyday wishes and casual memories spring from the root of her homesickness. I know this is true without her having to say anything to me. I hear myself tell stories about Rhode Island the same way.

"Mom, I have to go," I whisper, unlatching her arm from around my waist. "I have to find Ted."

Dee hears me. "Where is that son of mine?" she demands. "He'd been hotfooting to get over here to see Jenny Elwig and now there she is by herself, looking just as snide and snotty as her mother."

"Ted's our boy." Alexa sips her drink, careful that her coral lips don't press the rim of the glass. "He's playing it smooth." The women sigh with laughter. My gaze laps once more around the porch and then I retreat inside. The skin around my fingernails is chewed raw.

I check the den, filled mostly with men, some of whom are smoking Dad's nasty Colombian cigars. The fumes choke me even from the doorway. It's easy to tell the army men from the Zonians because the army men wear short sleeve shirts or T-shirts with their shorts or jeans but the Zonian men wear the traditional pleated and hand-smocked *guayabera* shirt, in either white or pale blue.

Turnip-nosed Captain Jacobs holds the floor. He reminds me of that part in the Santa Claus poem, about the smoke encircling his head like a wreath, except that Captain Jacobs never looks like a right jolly old elf; more like a right drunk jerk.

"I understand Carter wanting to phase it back to them eventually," he's puffing. "But why now, when they can't even pay out their debt to us? This country's so poor — it's never gonna cover upkeep of running the locks without our help."

The room fills with quarrelsome voices as everyone starts competing to explain their dumb old philosophies about the Canal; what it means to the world, who it really belongs to, blah blah blah.

I stand quietly and listen to this same old argument I've heard so many times since we moved here; who should control the Canal? Dad's quiet, too. He swallows long from his drink and then blinks down at it's surface, probably trying to figure out the right way to present his opinions; it's another way we're alike, I guess.

"Hey Dad," I call to him. He looks up to where I am haunting the doorway. For a moment his face is all bewildered, like he can't quite remember who I am. Then he frowns at me and mouths, "Go to bed."

"Dad have you seen —?"

"Now." He swings his arm loosely in my direction and his voice is loud enough to switch the focus of some of the others.

I give up and escape from the smoke and argument.

17

Marita sits in the one chair of her room off the kitchen, folding laundry. Her eyes are bloodshot and her hair is starting to slip out of its ponytail. I notice she changed back into her cut-off jeans shorts and tank shirt. Linda is lying on Marita's bed, asleep in her now crumpled beige uniform. When I enter her room after knocking, Marita touches a finger to her lips and tilts her head toward Linda.

"You are sunburned," Marita whispers. I bring my warm fingers to my warm face and nod. Even at night, the sun figures out a way to sneak into my skin.

"Hey," I say. "You should just do those clothes tomorrow. You look pretty tired."

Marita massages the corner of her eye. "*Tal vez,*" she says. "I am waiting for your brother to come home."

"How did you know he was gone?" I demand. "Did you see him leave?"

"Sshh," Marita hisses. "I see him just before and he says he forgot his shoes by the *bohío* you all are building."

"The war fort. He didn't go there, though. He went to Ninth Street to go fight some kid, like he said at dinner. Like I told you he was going to do at dinner." I can hear my voice accusing her.

"Well, what can I say when Charlie tells me he is back in fifteen minutes?" Marita hooks her hands together into her lap and her tired eyes fasten on me sternly. "You know this thing, you say nothing to Señor y Señora?"

I twitch my head up away from her gaze. "I wouldn't rat on Charlie."

"He will be home soon. You can wait with me if you want." she says. "But no jumping around the way you do, like a *loco* monkey. Makes me jump, too."

I try to relax and so I sit on the floor to do my meditating. Marita reaches down and turns on her standing floor fan. The breeze lifts the ends of my hair and cools my sunburn. Marita settles back in her chair and picks up her paperback from off the floor.

"What are you reading?" I ask her. "Another romance?"

"Mmm, a good one," she says. "Very — ah — with lots of love."

"Like, sumptuous, you mean?"

"I do not know this word," she murmurs. She reads intensely, like the words are a feast — I know how she feels, since I bet it's how I look when I read my Nancy Drews. I study the cover. The woman is very bosomy and the man behind her looks like he's biting her neck. It definitely looks very sumptuous. I just learned that word myself.

"I know a poem about winter," I say after a minute. I'm interrupting her reading but my meditating just seems to be making me more nervous. "Do you want to hear it?"

"*Claro.*" Marita fixes her gaze to me and tucks her knees up beneath her, and for the second time today, I recite my poem. When I'm finished Marita's face is just a blank.

"*Pues, entonces* . . . I never saw winter and snow," she says. "Except in movies."

"It's just a stupid nursery rhyme and sometimes it makes me sad but it feels good to say." I shrug.

Marita picks up her book and starts reading again, but when she feels me looking at her she waves it at me. "*Escucha* — I will read you this," she says. "Listen." Marita opens the book and reads out loud from it. The strange, Spanish words don't exactly stick to me, but when she is finished I'm quiet, because

Marita's eyes are far away, dreamy, and wistful like the girl on the cover of my journal. I wonder if she just read me a sexy part.

Linda's body stirs, as if she understands the sense of Marita's words even in her sleep.

"I only understand a little bit of Spanish." I confess what Marita already knows. "But I am going to try to learn more. I know more than Charlie, that's for sure."

"Maybe then you teach it to Charlie," Marita says. "He listens to you, sometimes."

Charlie. Where is he and where is Ted? Marita's room is beginning to feel way too warm.

"I need some water," I say, getting up from the floor.

"No running off to find him," Marita orders. "I don't need two missing. He will be back soon."

I close the door gently behind me. It hadn't occurred to me that I should run off to find him without Ted until Marita slipped the thought into my head. Now the idea gradually shifts through me and I move slowly, like a zombie, from the kitchen to the front door and step outside to the concrete steps. But I don't feel so good. My stomach's kinked with worry and the sunburn's heat on my face warms my cold fingertips. Maybe I really am sick. I wonder what the symptoms are for yellow fever.

Sounds of music and laughter from the house lap at me in waves. I look out over the yard, torn between the safe light leading to my house and the dim glow of the moon that might lead me to Charlie. Above me, a moth snaps into the small iron lantern that burns over our front door. I watch it until I can't anymore.

All at once, tiredness pours through me, heavy and gray as concrete. I am stopped by the feeling, by its thickening in my feet, my fingers, around my heart and lungs. I lift a bare foot off the step, surprised that I can move at all, amazed at how I can fill each minute with so much worry that I feel like I'm always drowning. It's a clear break of thought, and then the accident smashes through my mind in a thousand hurting pieces. I close my eyes but the noises don't end; the police and ambulance sirens, the shouts through the darkness, the screaming. Again I can feel the cold cold air, the horrible weight of a body crushed over me, and then lifted away.

I leap off the bottom stair and start running.

18

It's not so much that I know where Charlie would go as I can reason out what he wouldn't do. He wouldn't want to run down Main Street, but would try to cut through as many people's properties as he could, so that he could feel more covert and commando-ish. He also has less chance of being spotted and asked for ID by the night-patrolling MP's if he keeps away from the paved roads.

I turn off Third Street when I hit the top of the hill, then veer diagonally through Major Wimble's lawn and over to Fourth Street. Charlie wouldn't want to be close to the gatehouse of the base, because he has more chance of running into a parent who might telephone Mom and Dad about sighting one of their children on the loose. Charlie sightings, at odd hours in strange places, are commonly reported by Fort Bryan do-gooders. By staying over the hill and near the pit, where we know fewer people, he's better camouflaged.

I'm running fast, but my heart's pounding in sick, stop-motion thuds. I feel like I'm in one of those dreams where no matter how fast you run, your joints seem stuck and you know you can't get away from where you are — or get to where you need to be. Dr. Forrest says those dreams are common for people with chronic anxiety. My feet stub into unexpected rocks and sticks and I cry out in whisper-screams. The regular old sounds prickle me now; a shout, the slam of a screen door, the rustling of unseen enemies lurking in the trees.

Moonlight trickles weakly over the houses. A few have their porch and outside lights on, but pockets of black space seem to jump out in front of me. I just keep hoping that I won't trip over a lawn chair or a Big Wheel or something. Faceless commies could be hunched in the dark spaces, waiting for me, and I run faster, swallowing up the black night air. My dress keeps twisting up around my legs, and my feet throb every time they slap the ground.

My mind's whispering "Where is Charlie? Where is Charlie?" like a meditation chant, but I'm remembering something else, thinking back to this other night — it was when we lived in Rhode Island — and Charlie and I were playing food truth or dare.

Charlie dared me to eat a red pepper, chili sauce, and a crusty smear of horseradish, which he had mushed all together and spread on a saltine. When I first told him I wouldn't eat it, he said that he'd have to tell all the kids at school how I kissed and hugged my stuffed animals before I went to sleep.

"No fair!" I shouted. "That truth's too familyish!"

"Then you gotta take the dare, I guess. You must eat zee fire cracker!" He held his creation to my mouth — the cracker was so unfairly much worse than the spoon of coffee grounds and Crisco I had just made him swallow.

"Come on, Charlie." Frustrated tears welled up in my eyes. "Telling that's not even a choice for me."

"Sor-ry. One or the other," he taunted.

"That's so mean."

"That's life."

The saltine was so poison-hot that I bolted out of the house into the winter cold, and then, since it was dark and there was nowhere to go, I just kept running around and around the house, screaming, like I was in a cartoon. Every time I passed the kitchen window I could hear Charlie laughing. When I came inside, though, tears still streaming down my face from all those spices, I saw that Charlie had made another fire cracker, which he crammed into his mouth right in front of my eyes.

"Why are you doing that — don't do that!" I gasped. He howled like a dog and shot out the door, doing laps around the house like I just had, and that's when I started laughing. I laughed so hard I forgot how much my mouth burned. When he came back inside we both sat on the kitchen floor, rubbing our tongues with wet paper towels while laugh tears striped our cheeks.

But that was over two years ago, before the accident, when Charlie used to know how to undo his mean things. I don't even know why I'm thinking of that story now, except that I feel sort of the same way now as I did then, doing those laps around the house, running and running and mad at Charlie.

Past Fourth Street the base gets wider, and the neighborhoods are separated by flat fields instead of square, identical yards. The darkness becomes harder to understand or predict. I run through the flat spaces that divide Fifth and Sixth and Seventh streets; I've never pushed myself so far so fast and my worry pulses in every heartbeat and every uneven exhale of my breath.

Someone's approaching, running toward me in the dark; I hear the noise from a distance and then it's impossibly close. "Charlie!" I cry. "Is that you, Charlie?" I'm scared; *Please let it be Charlie*, I pray; but the figure that adjusts and takes shape in my eyes is too tall. It's some man, not Charlie. A freezing terror clenches me and I brake, spinning hard on my heel to sprint in the opposite direction.

"Lane, it's me. I found him." A pair of arms grabs me rough around the shoulders and wheels me around.

"Ted! You found him?" I have to work to register and connect to Ted's face, to calm myself.

"Yeah, yeah, but he's in bad shape."

"Charlie," I repeat. "He's okay?"

"Hang on a sec, Lane. What I'm trying to say is —"

"What — what *are* you saying?" I'm shivering and the sweat running down my arms and legs feels cold and slick. My knees buckle and I feel Ted wrenching me up, his hands hooked strong under my arms. He is pulling me up and shaking me.

"Listen," he says. I'm shivering so hard — I can't seem to stop shivering.

"Look up and listen, Lane, it's not that bad. At least, I don't know, but I don't think — stop shaking, Lane. You need to get hold of yourself. He's just off Ninth Street and he's — okay, he's a little messed up, okay? And I'm going to get my truck and I need you to help me out. Help me out. Are you listening to me? Are you listening?"

I make my eyes stare at Ted. His face looks gray

and damp; it could be shaped from clay, the way it appears under the moon.

"Where is he? I need to see him."

"That's right, okay, you need to go stay with him while I get the truck. I think his left leg's broken and he's missing some teeth, too, and I don't know what else, but look — hey are you listening to me?"

"I — yes, I'm listening. Where is he?"

"He's right off the road by the BQ. He wants me to get the truck and not tell your mom or dad or anyone, just get him to a doctor first."

"That's crazy. You know that's crazy."

"Listen to me. It's okay, it's Charlie being Charlie. So look, this is what I'm going to do. I'm going to get the truck and take him to the Fort Bryan clinic. We'll call the Duchess and whoever else once we get there. But we got to get him help fast. Are you listening?"

"I'm listening. I hear you."

"He's not winning any beauty contests right now." Ted half-laughs. "Lighten up, Lane, okay? Just try to act like everything's cool, like he's not as bad as he looks and most likely feels."

"Okay, okay. Let me go, I want to go."

"Then go, go." He shoves me in the direction of where he has come from and I start running, my fears replaced with purpose. I'm clenching my hands at my sides like Ginny Barker, the fastest girl runner in my grade, and my face feels smooth and determined as I sprint closer and closer to Charlie.

The BQ looks like a prison by night, dwarfing the smaller houses that stand on either side of it. A paper-shaded square of light through one of the BQ windows helps me to pick out my surroundings, but not enough to avoid the exposed drain pipe I accidentally crack my shin against. I fall to the ground with a yelp of pain.

"Lane!"

And then I see him.

19

His body's like a bent wire, twisted and leaning against the poured cement wall of the BQ.

"Hey!" I jump up and hobble closer to him, rubbing my shin. "I was so worried about you."

"That's a big surprise," Charlie sniffs. "So long as you didn't tell Mom."

"No, I didn't tell Mom or anyone. Will you tell me what happened?" I crouch next to him, touch the top of his head to make sure he's real. He looks up to stare at me and I have to fight to keep my expression calm.

Charlie's face looks like someone torch-blasted it open. Besides being scratched and dirty, blood and dirt are caked around the sides of his mouth. Fresh blood trickles from his gums, and I see dark pockets where teeth should be. Then I notice that one of his legs is bent out from the knee at an abnormal angle. When I touch it, he winces.

"Don't," he says.

"Ted's coming with the truck. He'll be here any minute."

"He's not telling Mom and Dad?"

"No. He says we'll get you to the clinic first thing and worry about the rest later. That's not your bad leg, is it?" I ask.

"Other one."

"That's some luck, I guess."

"Yeah." Charlie touches his hand to the side of his jagged mouth, gently pressing at the scraped puffy skin and the drying blood around his lips. When he talks more blood dribbles out of the corners of his mouth.

"What happened, anyway?"

"I must look pretty bad, the way you're staring at me."

"You don't look so bad now that I'm adjusted. What happened?"

He hesitates, like he's searching his memory. "Jason McCullough," he says finally.

"Are you kidding? You got in a fight with Jason McCullough? You found him? He was here with you?" I cannot believe it. And then I don't believe it.

"I got to the fort and started calling him." Charlie begins. I have to hold my breath to hear his voice. "I was calling out, like — 'Jason McCullough, you gonna hide in a tree your whole life, like a monkey? Or you gonna come down and fight the fight with me?' And I was making chicken noises — you know, stuff like that. And then I hear something in the tree like a whispering sound and I start getting more like, anxious, and so . . ." He stops and pushes the bottoms of his hands into his closed eye sockets. I can't tell if he's crying or just really tired.

"I think I scratched my eye." He speaks just on top of a whisper. "Something feels really weird in my eye, like dirt got in there."

"Ted'll be here any minute. Did you climb the tree?"

"So no — yeah, I shinnied up the trunk and got a leg up and when I got to the top there's this wood ledge and Jason McCullough was there and he punched me and grabbed my leg — my bad one — but I punched him back and he lost balance so he started, like, holding onto my other leg but I kicked him in the face and he let go. That's when he fell. When I climbed down from the tree, though, he was gone."

I make my face a mask of concern, but specks of doubt are stirring up in my brain, as I try to grab hold of this crazy old image of Charlie battling Jason McCullough, who keeps flipping back and forth in my memory; sometimes in a soccer uniform with a bowl hair cut, then as a pair of sneakers in a tree.

"We'll get you to a doctor, Charlie. Someone to fix you up." I flatten over my doubts with my confident older-sister voice.

"I just wish Ted would hurry," he sighs. "I'm hurting all over."

It seems like hours before Ted's truck pulls up to the BQ. He jumps down from the driver's side and runs to Charlie, hoisting Charlie up in his arms with a mild, "Easy does it, Charleston."

I follow. In the shadowy dashboard window I see Marita's face, eyes dark and glittering as a stray cat's but a million times more comforting.

She climbs out and takes Charlie from Ted with capable arms.

"I'm too heavy," Charlie insists.

"Lucky for you I ate my fruit this morning," Marita answers him. Charlie laughs, thankfully.

"You think something got punched up inside him?" I whisper to Ted as Marita slides into the passenger seat, Charlie cradled in her arms.

"We'll make the doctors take x-rays," he answers. "Everything's fine now that we've got him."

I wonder if Ted can see how nothing's ever exactly fine with old Charlie, that no doctor's going to be able to find Charlie's broken parts in an x-ray or stitch him back together so that he doesn't want to rip himself up again. I wish Ted could see. I'm getting tired of being the only smart pair of eyes watching Charlie.

I try to get rid of these pointless thoughts before they upset me too much.

"Lane, are you okay alone back in the flatbed? We're just going a short ways."

"I'm good."

"Hang on, then."

I hold its edges as the truck gathers speed once we are off Ninth Street and onto Main Road. I wonder what Mom and Dad are doing, if they noticed that we're gone. I guess they would just think we were sleeping at the Davidson's, if anyone bothered to check.

I notice first. The clinic's closed. There's only enough amber light shining over the glassed-in reception area to show that it's empty. I reach my arm around to tap the side of Ted's door as he wheels the truck around. He leans out.

"Plan B," he says. He speaks tightly. "McKenna clinic. Okay?"

"Good thinking."

Ted drives way too fast now, whipping down the road and off-base. McKenna will actually be better; more like a real hospital with an emergency room staff, I remember all the helpful starched people from that time when Charlie stepped on a broken root beer bottle and had to have six stitches in his ankle.

Then, in a flash, I remember and I start pounding on the window.

"Ted, we can't — Ted we're not —" I'd forgotten, since we'd been traveling on and off-base so much today. I pound on the roof of the truck cab although I know it's too late; we have already turned off-base a few miles ago.

The truck slams to a stop on the side of the road. I hear Ted curse and pound his fists on the steering wheel. He's figured it out, too. He presses his fanned fingers over his face and mutters something I can't hear. Then Charlie is yelling, "Forget it Ted, you're not calling anyone, figure out something else" — while Marita jabbers over him, yelling *"¿Qué pasa?*, What's the problem, what? What?"

"We don't have a pass!" I call out. "Without a pass, we can't get back onto another base."

There are no streetlights on the roads separating the bases; I squint my eyes and see nothing but shadows and the border of the jungle. Charlie's head drops onto Marita's shoulder and I can hear Marita speaking Spanish to Ted; with the finger of one hand she draws a sort of map or diagram in the palm of the other. Ted nods occasionally. I watch his face in profile; his mouth jiggles a frilly toothpick — probably from our house — up and down. Then he leans out the driver's side window.

"We're going to *Viejo Abaja*, to *Santo Cristóbal* — it's a hospital. Marita says it's fine, they'll be able to fix Charlie up, no problem." I can tell from his voice that he's not convinced that this plan is all that great.

"Isn't there a clinic on the Zone? There's got to be something else," I plead. "There has to be."

"Too far to drive across the isthmus. *Cristóbal* isn't too far; it's just downtown a ways." Ted turns the ignition; his mind's made up. Charlie doesn't speak a word against the plan since Mom and Dad still aren't involved in it, and so I'm silent. I've never seen a downtown hospital, but I imagine cracked concrete floors and exposed lightbulbs and mean-faced old Spanish-gibbering nurses. *Santo Cristóbal*. It sounds scary.

Ted turns the engine over and the truck lurches forward. I wonder what he's thinking; Ted, who thinks that all locals are out to steal and swindle the Zonians, now having to drive downtown to get help from them. I'm scared for Charlie and me, too. What if we get to the hospital and people start shouting, "Gringos go home!" I feel sick to my stomach, thinking about it.

We turn onto the *Tumba Muerto* and then swerve onto the underpass, under the bright cigarette billboard, and through to a part of the highway I've never seen, never thought I'd see. *Peligroso*, even Marita is quick to warn. Not the right place to be driving at night.

The road's empty, though, except for a few smelly eighteen-wheeler trucks. Many of the highway street-lights are smashed, but there's enough light from the moon to read the highway signs and the white lines in the road. I bet it's way after midnight by now.

Marita points out directions as we keep exiting and getting on different little stretches of the highway, until we have turned onto a lifeless section of down-town, the other end from where I've ever been when Mom and Alexa take me shopping. This section is darker; there are no shops, only dark rows of jammed-together old buildings. The air is weighted with dirty smells of exhaust fumes and rotten fruit. I try not to breathe too much. I don't like the idea of breathing up anything more than pure air.

I see a dog, his stomach stretched bone-skinny, snuffling at a plastic bag on the side of the road. A woman, wearing a pink dress even brighter than Alexa's lipstick, is leaning in the door of a red-lit bar. A car pulls up from behind, its radio turned on loud enough to frighten me, and it's windows are blacked out so I can't tell who's riding inside it. I wonder if I'm safe, out here in the nasty open air in the back of

Ted's truck. Locals shoot at MP's all the time — to them, I'd probably pass as target practice.

When *Santo Cristóbal* looms up in front of us, looking more like a church than a hospital, I try to resist jumping out of the moving truck and running the rest of the way. A stone statue of Balboa, standing with his sword drawn at the gate entrance, seems both comforting and fearsome. Marita jumps out of the truck before any of us, Charlie heavy in her arms as she lugs him to the emergency room door. She's shouting in Spanish. I recognize the words *help* and *child*, but that's all.

Lights burst forward with the swinging doors, a group of people dressed in green shirts and pants swoop down on little Marita, and I watch as Charlie is picked up and thrust inside on one of those metal wheely beds. Ted and I jog behind, into the bright lights and uniforms and toy-colored plastic furniture of the emergency waiting room. Marita is already speaking to a man — a doctor, I guess — who jots words quickly on his chart. The doctor touches Charlie's leg and shines a pricking light into Charlie's blood-crumbly mouth. Then he pries Charlie's hand away from his eye to squint in there, too. He speaks softly to Charlie, who keeps his face in one expression, trying to be tough.

I bet he's thinking, "Indians don't cry, Indian's

don't cry," which is what Emily and Charlie and I always used to say to each other if one of us got hurt, to force ourselves to be tougher. A long time ago, Emily had read somewhere that Indians never show emotion in public, and we all decided this was pretty cool. Later, when Charlie and I were in the hospital together, we would whisper it to each other. Charlie looks at me now.

"Indians." He rolls his eyes. I know what he means — even if you don't want to think, "Indians don't cry," every time you're in pain, you just end up thinking it and then it's like you *have* to be like an Indian. I have the exact same problem.

"Heya, Ted," Charlie whispers. He sticks his hand out from under the cover and swipes at Ted's arm. "You come in with me? Lane's a wimp about blood, of course."

"You know it, Charleston. I'm going to have to back up your Lightning Gods story, right?"

"Yeah." Charlie laughs. I wonder what's with Ted and this Lightning God thing. It must be some weird Zonie legend. Zonie's all seem to like lies and legends more than religion, even if they're technically Jewish or Catholic or whatever.

"Call the Duchess," Ted orders. He fishes deep in his pocket and shakes a mound of silver change into my hand. "And get yourself and Marita a drink or something."

" 'Bye, Lane." Charlie coughs as he is wheeled down the hall.

"He's okay." Ted's voice is firm. Marita and I wait until they disappear around the corner before we return to the waiting room. I find the phones in the corner.

I pick up the receiver and slide a dime into the box to dial home. The connection's awful — the roar of a noise that sounds like the ocean almost drowns out the ringing; once, twice, three times. I count to fifteen before hanging up.

There's an ancient-looking vending machine standing beside the phone. I feed change into the mouth of the machine, pressing the buttons for a candy bar, but I do the numbers wrong and the machine drops a package of popcorn instead. I buy two colas for Marita and me, and there's still change to drop in my pocket.

I tear open the popcorn as I walk back to the line of connecting chairs where Marita sits and offer the cola and bag to her. She pops the can and digs out a handful of popcorn.

"*¿Vienen el Señor y la Señora?*"

"No, I couldn't get hold of anyone. The party must be too loud or something."

"Ay — so many people, what a mess." She knuckles her hand to her chin and we sit, drinking our colas and passing the bag of popcorn between us. It's stale and the kernels creak as I chew them into my back teeth. Salty, too.

"We'll need the right car to get back on base," I mention. "I don't know what we're going to do if we can't get hold of Mom and Dad, and I feel weird about calling up their friends. I mean, it's so late and everything."

"*No te preocupes.* Don't worry." She yawns. I slide back and I close my eyes.

When Charlie and I were in a hospital together, last time, I had liked the curtain divider all the way closed and Charlie liked it half-closed, and we kept yanking it back and forth between us, not talking but both of us just listening to the jingle of the curtain rungs. Back and forth, back and forth, it would move, until one nurse on duty threatened to move me down the hall.

We stopped yanking the curtain after that, switching the battle to clicking our remote controls to the shared television back and forth to different channels. Click, click, click, neither of us saying a word to the other. Sometimes the fights would drag on so long that they were almost funny. Fighting with Charlie is one thing I've always counted on to make me feel really intense, really alive. He sure knows how to get to me.

Marita sits down next to me. "*Dios mío*, I hate hospitals."

"Me too." I close my eyes and yawn, wishing for bed. Marita nudges me.

"Five to win," she says. She throws a piece of popcorn from her last handful up in the air and catches it neatly with a crocodile snap of her mouth. I try to copy her but mine bounces off my nose and under my feet. Marita flicks up another piece, and again, another perfect catch. Two to zero.

"Keep on your eye," she instructs, pointing to her own eye. I flip up a kernel, open my eyes wide, and it drops squarely into my mouth.

"*Perfecto.*" Marita claps. "*¡Fabuloso!*" She throws her next piece a good three feet into the air and it dive bombs right in.

"*Fabuloso,*" I laugh. What a Charlie game — fun and stupid, and of course there's no way I'll win. My next piece lands in my hair. She beats me five to two.

Marita folds the bag into a square once it's empty and then saves the square in the pocket of her jeans shorts; why, I don't know, but I don't ask.

20

We doze in the waiting room for over an hour before Ted appears.

"Well, it's a nice messy break, Charlie style," he informs us with a tired smile. He rubs his fingers over his eyebrows so that they bristle up. "And, for our side dishes, we have bruised ribs and a split lip. I wouldn't recommend the oral surgery tonight, but the scraped —"

"Okay, that's enough. I don't think I can listen to all the details." I put my hand on my stomach. "As long as he's going to be all right."

"He's okay. Nothing that won't heal. Come on and see for yourself."

Marita and I follow Ted down the hall and up a flight of stairs. This hospital doesn't look too different from an army one; just shabbier. The walls are dark mustardy colored, though; not white, and the scarred linoleum floor curls up where it meets the wall. Still, it reminds me of a regular hospital in that every molecule of air I inhale smells like the word *sick*.

Ted nods to a couple of nurses standing together at the other end of the hall and pushes a door open. The room is windowless and the boxed air is a bad mixture of vinegar and air freshener smells. Charlie lies propped up on the one narrow bed; chin down, arms crossed, and shoulders hunched up high enough to touch his ears. His ankle-to-thigh leg cast, in the uneven light, throws a chunky shadow on the wall.

"Six weeks of this monster." Ted walks to the foot of the bed and raps the plaster with his knuckles. "Charleston, you're sure not built for speed right now." Marita makes a soft clucking sound and presses her hand on Charlie's cheek. He flinches.

"Don't," he says. "I hurt too much."

I move closer to the bed and curl my hands around its scratched metal side bar, leaning closer to study Charlie as if he's an exhibit at the zoo. He raises his head and looks at me hard. He's wearing a silver metal cup that looks like a sieve taped over one eye, and a couple of black stitches have taken over his top lip.

"Zorro." I point. "You have a mustache."

"Ted says I'll have a mean scar." Charlie looks at Ted, who nods.

"Like a pirate. Charlie Hook." Ted's smile turns

into a yawn. "Okay guys, I'm heading back to the Zone to trade the truck for Dee's car with the pass sticker. Then I'll cruise back and pick up the three of you. It'll be a while. Are you cool to hang out?" I give him the thumbs-up. He waves, and we watch him go. Marita hovers a minute, then she leaves, too, drawn out to the hall by the sound of Spanish-speaking nurses.

"I come back," she says vaguely. "Just be out here."

"Do the light, Lane?" Charlie asks when it's just us. I flip off the light switch, relieved at the darkness that fills the ugly bareness of the room.

"I never got hold of Mom and Dad." I sit carefully on the edge of Charlie's bed. "No one was answering the phone. What are you going to tell them when we get home?"

"Something. I'm still thinking of the right story."

"It makes the bike accident last month look like nothing."

"Yeah, this is something."

"Sure is. Something else."

We are quiet together for a long time, so long that I think he has fallen asleep, and when he breaks the silence, I'm startled and I realize I must have been half asleep, too.

"Lane, you think I'm crazy?"

I think about all the people I know who are crazy.

There's old Mrs. Hibbits, who lives in a big spooky house near Mina and Pops and who lurks in a shrunken shadow behind her mildewed kitchen curtains. She'll be silent for hours and then suddenly yell, "Everybody get away! And no bikes on my lawn!" even if it's only you, without a bike, walking on the sidewalk not anywhere near her lawn. Definitely crazy is Michael Ambrosia in my grade, who staples the wings of moths and butterflies together and once even stapled the skin of his own two fingers to each other, but I was out sick that day; Steph had to phone me and squeal all about each disgusting detail. And you can't forget those crazies you read about, like the man who lives in a house with no food and fifty-six dogs until the Humane Society finds out, and then you see his picture in the paper and think, *Would I have known he was crazy if I'd bumped into him on the street?*

"No, you're not crazy, Charlie," I tell him. "You've just been in a bad mood for a while is all."

"Sometimes I feel crazy," he says. "Because I think I have a certain feeling in common with crazy people."

"A feeling like what?"

"A feeling that nothing's too scary. Nothing, not one single thing is *too* scary to see, or do, or find out about. So you might as well try it. You know what I mean?"

"I guess," I say slowly. "But it's hard for me to know *exactly*, since I'm scared of everything."

"I don't know if that's so great either." Charlie sighs. "Ted was cool through the whole time in the emergency room. He just kept cracking jokes, making me laugh. I kind of hope he'll stop calling me Charleston, though. Charlie Hook's a little better."

"He likes renaming people." I grin.

"No, not everyone. Just our family," Charlie points out. "You know, this might sound weird and sort of — I don't know, but sometimes, like today when we were driving in the truck and getting the wood for the fort and stuff, I was sort of pretending a little that he was my older brother."

"Sometimes, in a way, I do that too," I admit. Charlie smiles, and looks relieved. "But I mean, I don't necessarily think it's a bad thing; in a way it's lucky for us. To have an older brother. I mean, it's not a replacement for anything, it's just Ted, it's who he is."

"Right." Charlie agrees. He coughs and stares up at the ceiling and he twists up the covers around and around in his fingers. His body is tense by the thoughts pressing out from inside him. Once he opens his mouth and then closes it into a frown. "Lane, I need to break the rule, okay?" he says finally. "Just for a couple minutes."

"Well, I won't tell."

"Oh gee thanks, considering you break it like every second . . ."

"I won't — I mean . . . I want to hear it. A lot, I do."

"Honestly, Lane. If Mom and Dad knew how much you broke it, even though you think you have it all worked out saying —"

"Do you want to tell me something or not?" I ask. My voice hurts my throat; I try to relax.

"I just wanted to ask you a question is all. Okay?"

"Fine."

"Then okay, what's the worst for you?"

I pull one leg up so that my foot rests on the edge of the bed and I balance my chin on my knee. Keeping my mouth shut, I snap my teeth open and closed and listen to the amplified click of my jawbone in my ears. I listen to the clicking for a long time; I try to pace it to my heartbeat.

"Tell me," says Charlie.

"Well, I guess being the oldest now is worst for me. I'm not very good at it; I don't know — maybe I can't ever feel old enough."

"You sure worry a whole lot. You're old as an old granny," he assures me.

"I'm getting better. About the worrying."

"Yeah, well, you can't get much worse."

"I was worse last year, Dr. Forrest said."

"Forehead — all that Forehead tried to do was

make me cry. No thanks. I can use my eyes for better things than that." Charlie's voice is all tough, but I wonder.

"I think she was just doing the best she could, considering Mom and Dad are both pathological liars, with their rules about the accident and everything."

"What's a pathological liar?"

"It's like a person who tries to make their lie the truth." I hesitate. "It's like a disease."

"Well, the worst for me is —" Charlie offers, but then he's quiet again for a long time before he speaks. "I think the worst for me is remembering those pictures over and over in my head, the ones from the insurance company of the ice on the side of the road and the tree and our car and everything. And I wonder how could Mom and Dad and you and me've all been in that same smashed-up car and be okay? And sometimes I wish, I mean, what I *think* I wish, is that it had been all of us, instead of one, just one, you know? Like the peaches."

It takes me a minute to understand what Charlie's talking about and then I slide closer to lie down next to him. My head rests on the edge of his pillow and our legs and waists and shoulders are even with each other. Not quite touching, but we are close enough so that the touch lies in the short space between us. He doesn't say anything, but he stops knotting up the covers in his fingers. We lie quietly like that for a while.

"When you'd leave the room to look for her, when we were back in the hospital." I am speaking so quietly it's like I'm not speaking at all. "I'm sorry I couldn't — I didn't go with you."

"It's 'cause you *knew*, Lane," Charlie answers. He keeps staring at the ceiling. "You were sitting right in the middle between us in the car, so you must've . . . and I really just . . . thought I'd find her and, you know, bring her back to our room to be with us. I guessed she was probably all scared, being by herself, or with some weird roommate, so I kept going down the hall, looking into other people's rooms and they'd be getting shots or resting or whatever." He smiles, remembering. "And that Nurse Fatty with the nose hair'd catch me and haul me back."

"So you'll remember what Jason McCullough looks like tomorrow?"

He turns his head away from the ceiling. The silver cup over his eye looks like a million tiny eyes staring at me.

"Aw, Lane. I just fell is all. I climbed too high in that stupid tree and I lost my balance. I kept thinking that if I climbed higher I'd find the dumb kid, that he was just outside my reach. Only the higher I climbed, the less I saw, and the branches got narrower and narrower, and then I fell." He grins crookedly through his punched-out teeth. "So hey, I'm an idiot, right?"

"I won't tell."

"You never tell."

Then I think back again to when Charlie dared me to eat the fire cracker, and I wonder if he really would have told everyone how I kissed my stuffed animals. "Hey Charlie, remember the time —"

"Listen," Charlie says softly as he puts his finger against his lips. "I think I hear Ted."

We're silent and then we hear Ted's too-loud self filling the hall. He starts up an energetic discussion with Marita and one of the nurses. I listen to the thick barrier of their Spanish, dented here and there by the words I know — *car, going, I hope* — not enough for me to figure out the conversation, although I try. A few moments later Ted bursts into the dark room.

"You guys know what time it is?" he asks. "Try four-thirty in the morning! Pretty good, wouldn't you say? I know I'm getting a second wind — ready for a little road trip, in fact, if you two'd care to join?"

"Four-thirty in the morning," I repeat with disbelief. "I don't think I've ever been awake this late."

"First time for everything." Ted points gun fingers at me. "Okay, Charleston, heave-ho. I'm sure you're the chief on crutches, but let me just carry you out to

Dee's beautiful Thunderbird which, I gotta tell you, is a strange beast to drive. Lane, you get the crutches?" He slides his arms under Charlie, folding him up against his chest. I stand up from the bed; my feet have pins and needles and I stomp around the room to get the blood rushing back through them.

Outside the hospital, a man is just starting to unload a truck full of pastries and dark homemade bread, setting up his stand for the morning. It's the kind of bread Mom always buys from downtown, so with the rest of Ted's change, I buy a loaf.

Marita stays with Charlie in the back seat as we drive out of downtown. Something about this time between night and day seems mystical and secret, probably because I'm never awake to see it. The purple morning light is just beginning to break through the darkness. I unroll my window and breathe in the clean morning mist, then lean back in my seat and close my eyes, lulled by the leisurely drone of the car's engine. Midway home I hear Charlie at my back, snoring lightly.

The MP on duty gives us a brittle little salute and nod as we roll through the entrance gates of Fort Bryan. Ted salutes back.

21

The house is dark and messy and still. We whisper good night to Marita, who slips into her room. As she closes her bedroom door, Marita touches my cheek. "*Buenas noches, una niña bonita.* You are a good sister." She pulls the door shut and I hear the click of its lock.

With Ted behind me holding Charlie, I pick our path through the stray pieces of furniture and discarded cups and dinner plates, up the stairs to his bedroom. But when I open Charlie's door to the roar of the air-conditioner, I see a long body rolled up like a caterpillar under the blue-and-white-striped covers of his bed. I signal for Ted to stop in the doorway as I creep closer to get a better look.

"Mom?"

Her eyes lift slowly from their burdened sleep. I see

a web of red veins mapped through them. "Lanie? How was the Davidsons'? Isn't it still really early?"

"Why are you in here?" I whisper.

"Daddy was snoring. Is Charlie still at the Davidson's?"

"Why aren't you in the guest room?"

"Alexa's in there." Mom yawns and tries to prop up her head a little, but then she slowly sinks back into the sheets. "I'm just resting," she yawns, then she squeezes her eyes tight.

"Mom, can you hear me?" I whisper louder, but she just smiles.

"I'm listening," she murmurs, and then the smile fades away from her mouth as she disappears back into sleep.

I am still holding the loaf of bread which I forgot to put in the kitchen, and so I place it on the pillow next to Mom for her to see when she wakes up later in the morning. She lies on her back, and her sleep is solid and lifeless.

I walk back to Ted and Charlie. "Late night for the Duchess, eh?" Ted grins. "Let's put him in your room."

"Then where do I sleep?" I hiss, but he's already down the hall and through the next door into my room, where he plunks Charlie on my bed. I lean the crutches in the corner. Ted brushes his hands together.

"Sleep tight," he orders, looking down on Charlie. "I'm going home. I'm dead on my feet."

" 'Night, Ted," Charlie mutters, half-asleep.

On the way out my door, Ted messes my hair with both his hands. I try to duck him off.

"Thanks for all your driving and help," I say awkwardly. "You're pretty cool to do all that."

"Cool as Nancy Drew?" he asks.

"Well, no." I smile. "But pretty cool."

"See you later." He laughs and winks at me. I watch the back of his head as he thumps down the stairs, and then I run to my window to watch him get into Dee's Thunderbird, back it out of the carport, and drive away.

I click on my air-conditioner and sit on the edge of my bed, and look over to check on Charlie. His chest rises and falls in sleep breaths. He reminds me of a Frankenstein monster, with his heavy white cast and black stitches and that spooky silver eye cup. Tomorrow he'll sure have some explaining to do, and Mom and Dad will be extra high-strung if Alexa's eyes are present, feasting on the whole scene. Poor old Charlie. He always has some explaining to do.

Soon my room is frosted up with the Freon particles. I walk over to my desk and pick up my letter to

Emily and then I carefully pull open my desk drawer and drop the letter into the pile of all my other letters to Emily, all sealed in their envelopes and addressed with only her name in my perfect calligraphy.

A thought clicks inside my head, restless; it makes me move before I can even really think it through. I lift my desk chair and tiptoe out of my room, down the hall, and through my parent's bedroom, where Dad's snoring like a sad giant. I move cautiously, although I know almost nothing wakes Dad up when he snores that way, and I open the door to the walk-in closet, holding my breath against the creak I know it makes.

I snap on the closet light with my shoulder, then set down the chair and climb on top of it, reaching my arms high above me, up to the shelf of sweaters and tennis rackets, my hands groping but knowing, until I grasp Dad's old combat boot box. I pull it down. Carefully. Then I fold myself into a pretzel on the chair with the box resting on my lap, and I stare at the box, holding my breath, not moving, and all of a sudden a little scared.

Dad's snoring rumbles in a rhythm. I stroke and tap the sides of the box, uncertain. But then my fingers move ahead of my brain. They unpeel the gummed layers of Scotch tape securing the top of the box to its bottom, and then they shake off the cover. And for a moment I can't move, can't even breathe from the shock of seeing my sister again.

So many pictures. Her school pictures, her summer pictures, her snipped halves and quarters of pictures, some are just the tiniest sliver where Mom trimmed Emily from a background or a corner. And as my eyes are staring so fiercely over images I have never forgotten, just buried, I remember back to another dark day, when Charlie and I came home from school to find Mom sitting in the middle of the living room rug with these same shreds of photos scattered all around her, scissors still in her hand. Her eyes were so blank and disbelieving that I called Dad at work and told him to hurry up and come home.

No one's seen those pictures since that day; it was Dad who actually gathered them up and buried them in his combat boot box and started all the rules of no more talking and no more pictures. But now, looking over so many years of Christmases and birthdays, I'm just smiling and smiling and my memories fill to over-flowing inside me.

I search and dig out my favorite. I'm lucky that Mom left this one in one piece, not just with me in the front with a cut of nothing behind me. I'd forgotten that Emily's smile had that gap between her two front teeth and that her one hand — the one not holding the hair-spray bottle — is sort of draped around my shoulders.

"Dahling, you must stop by my saloon!" I read out loud. I soak up this picture for a long time and then I close my eyes, trying to feel the weight of Emily's arm resting on my shoulders again. I stare and stare until I feel my nose and mouth get warm and salty and my eyes hurt from not blinking, only I'm happy; I really am, just seeing her again.

It only takes me a minute to decide. I slide the photograph into the pocket of my sundress and then I pause, thinking. In another moment, I have found a second picture, my favorite of Emily and Charlie. I'd taken it myself, of the two of them standing in front of the Fort Lowthrop pool. Emily is wearing her ugly lily pad pattern bathing suit that she loved. It's an old picture, but I bet Charlie will remember it, because it was taken the day he got his Intermediate Otter swimming badge. He'd been pretty proud of himself that day. I unbend myself, replace the cover of the box and push it deep into its hiding place. I wobble slowly back down the hall with the chair, back into my bedroom with it, very slow, so as not to make any noise.

Mindful not to disturb Charlie, I hold my breath as I slide under the covers, but he doesn't move, just sleeps on like a lunk.

"Good night, Charlie," I say softly, placing my hand on his chest for a moment, just to make sure that he's breathing okay. He is. I throw the bedspread over us and close my eyes but I don't fall asleep all at once. My thoughts drift and settle like snow over all the different images now fresh in my mind. I tuck a corner of Charlie's picture just under the edge of his cast, so he'll be sure to see it when he wakes up. Then I sneak one more look at Emily and me, before I rest my own picture carefully over my heart like a shield to guard my memories. It feels good and solid there.

"*Bonita,*" I whisper.

Author's Note

Known also as the "Big Ditch," the Panama Canal measures approximately fifty-one miles from the Atlantic to the Pacific shoreline. Thousands of ships use the canal annually at a rate of nearly thirty-four vessels a day, making it a vital international throughway.

The territory of the Canal Zone came into existence in 1903 as a result of a treaty that, in exchange for a $10 million down payment and an additional $250,000 a year, gave the United States full power and control over the daily operations of the Panama Canal. By 1977, nearly 39,000 American citizens lived in the Panama Canal Zone; 9,000 of them were military personnel. Right from its inception, U.S. control of the canal became a symbol of imperial rule and a relic of the colonial era which was embarrassing not just for Panamanians, but for all Latin American countries.

In 1977 Panamanian general Omar Torrijos and U.S. president Jimmy Carter negotiated treaties calling for full Panamanian control over the canal and the Canal Zone by the year 2000. In 1979, the zone was abolished and the United States returned over half of the zone to Panamanian jurisdiction. Panama will take full control of its canal on December 31, 1999.

A. G.